Hardcore Erotic Story Stories

Explicit Adult Fantasies featuring Gangbangs, Threesomes, Domination, Lesbian, BDSM, Taboo, First Time, Anal, Role Play, Cuckold, BIPOC & MILFs

Jade St. James

Contents

Introduction

Dear friends,

Have you noticed, like I have, the explosion of erotic literature in the last few years?

I had been sharing these stories with friends online for a decade, but when I started to put them out there for the public, I realized... there was a genuine hunger for new and exciting sexy stories.

So, I've been soliciting stories from my favorite writers and putting them together for your enjoyment.

This time, I asked my writers to explore the world of "hardcore" sex. I wanted them to push their creative limits.

And WOW, did they deliver! This collection has some genuinely kinky and titillating themes that I know you'll enjoy!

And since this is a collection of short stories (my favorite format for erotic literature) if one story doesn't click with you, no problem! Just move on to the next one. But, I promise, if you dig in, you'll find new things you didn't know would turn you on.

And, I wanted to let you know I've integrated some of your feedback! I learned that many of you enjoy stories from both a man's and a woman's perspective - so this is evenly divided between male and female writers. (And narrators for the audiobook.)

So, sit back, relax, and enjoy this new "hardcore" collection. You won't regret it.

XOXO,
Jade

Rich Rick
by Shoshana Loy

August 15

"How's your sugar daddy?" Janet asks.

I roll my eyes.

She's talking about my boyfriend, Rick.

Or, as Janet calls him, Rich Rick. He's my sugar daddy, and I met him over the summer at an alumni event for the college. I'm 22 and highly attracted to the forty-two-year-old man.

Yes. Sex is involved. I know people think he's taking advantage of me, but he's not. Plus, the financial help is beyond rewarding.

Numbers and money is Janet's niche. She wants to be a financial advisor.

We attend college in Charleston, South Carolina,

and it is not cheap. The semester just started, and money is tight.

I am sitting at the kitchen table with Google Sheets open. My best friend/roommate, Janet, is talking about how we need a financial plan for the semester.

We discuss how much money I make monthly with my on-campus job compared to what my bills are. I explain that Rick has paid $500 for my books, and he gives me $1,500 a month. That's not a lot to others, but as broke college students, it's enough.

I tell Janet how much money I want in my savings by the end of the semester, and we start planning.

August 16

Rick and I have agreed on me coming to his place tomorrow to study.

Now that I'm older, I know that 42 is still young, and his energy proves it. Rick is vibrant, youthful, stern, and business-focused.

I enjoy being around him, but the money and gifts fuel our relationship. He takes me on shopping sprees and has gifted me with Balenciaga, Telfar, and Burberry.

He owns a warehouse that manufactures goods, and he makes $200,000 a year. After taxes, that is over

$6,000 a month. He is almost done paying off his million-dollar house. It is located outside of downtown Charleston. The five-bedroom and four-bathroom space is too big for one person, but he has visitors every month.

I was nosy when I asked him about his salary, but I needed to know how he could afford to live and give me $1,500 a month. I know he could probably give me more, but I can do so much with that amount.

He has a new Mercedes Benz. Over the summer, I drove his other car, a BMW, when mine was broken down. He wanted to buy me a new one, but I told him I didn't need people to see me with a new car.

August 17

"I wanted to run something by you," he said. "You and I haven't traveled together yet, and I hope we can in the future."

We are in his kitchen eating the breakfast he cooked.

"You're keeping me around for a while, I see," I say.

"I don't just throw women out when I'm tired of them," he said. "And this trip is for Europe next summer."

I don't mean for my jaw to drop to the floor, but I am ecstatic. I have been wanting to go to the United Kingdom for many years now. I make a mental note to make sure to give him *Thank you for Europe* sex.

I am trying to figure out what I did to deserve that type of trip.

"But there is one stipulation," he tells me.

I knew this trip had strings attached.

"I'm all ears," I said, sipping my juice.

I am okay with a stipulation because he is a businessman. They are full of loopholes, negotiations, and stipulations.

"I've been wanting to see you fuck multiple men."

I stop eating and look at him.

"What the fuck, Rick? A gangbang?"

"Yes, a gangbang," he says in a cool manner.

"What's going on, Rick? This isn't like you," I tell him. "Me fucking someone else other than you?"

"Let me explain," he says, pushing his food to the side. He puts all of his attention on me.

"You'd better motherfucking explain," I say, looking into his eyes.

"My friends and I have shared women in the past. It's always been nice, intimate moments. Not like what you see in pornos. These are debonair men who will take care of you and take you to bliss."

"But why me?"

"I know you're into trying new things and meeting new people," he tells me.

"Yes, for networking purposes and experiences for the 'Gram. Not to share my body with my rich boyfriend and his friends."

"But this is for Europe. You talk about visiting the UK one day."

"But not like this," I tell him. "You and I have this partnership because it is exclusive. You stopped talking to other women. I stopped talking to other men to do this relationship with you. Aren't I too young for a gangbang, anyway? Aren't I supposed to save that for when I'm in my 30s and bored as a wife or mother?"

I can see he is mulling things over in his head.

I continue to remind him that for these last four months, it has been just us. I emphasize that I've felt like we didn't need other people in the bedroom.

"I don't need an answer today," he finally says. "I picked these three men specifically because they have done this with me before. It was my then-girlfriend's idea. I just wanted the same experience with you."

"It's going to be hard to not think about this while studying."

A look of guilt hits his face. "I shouldn't have brought it up. I'll set up the atmosphere for you to study. Choose which room you want to study in, and I'll fix it up for you."

"No. I'm good. I'm leaving."

I gather my things and leave.

August 18

My phone is ringing, and I answer when I see it's Rick.

He's been apologizing for the last few days. While he apologized, I thought things over.

"How have you been?"

We make small talk, but my mind is on the gangbang.

"What are you getting out of seeing me with multiple men?" I inquire.

"You are fulfilling a fantasy that I've chased these last few years. I enjoy bringing my well-seasoned sexcapades to you. I would like to see you have another man inside of you beside me. And I want to be able to come inside you last."

My face gets hot, and I am sure my cheeks are pink. He mentioned coming inside of me because I like to watch creampie videos on my phone.

Rick is a stickler about us wearing a condom during sex.

I prefer raw sex and him coming inside of me

Rick greeted them once we were at the bottom of the stairs.

I was getting hot in the robe, and I felt like I was going to throw up.

"This is the woman of the hour," he said to them. "We're going to take care of her. We may be treating her like a whore tonight, but she is not one."

If my eyes could shoot daggers, Rick would be on the floor dead. Why mention whores at all?

"To make things less awkward, Rick set up a few things for you," Benny said.

There was a big quilt I loved to snuggle in on the floor, my favorite wine was chilling next to the blanket, and my favorite body oil was waiting for me.

Terrence grabbed my hand and led me to the blanket. Henry took my robe off, and Benny poured me a glass of wine.

I'm not a curvaceous woman. I have a small ass, but my breasts make up for it. I knew I looked good naked, but I was still anxious about being naked around them.

The men undressed, and I watched.

My goodness! Washboard abs were there. I wasn't sure if my mouth or kitty cat could handle their anacondas. The men weren't even fully hard, and I knew I was about to deal with nine inches each.

Terrence poured oil into his hands and rubbed them together as Benny started kissing me. I felt like I was tasting the sweetest strawberries on his lips. Terrence rubbed the slippery substance over and under my breasts, to my flat stomach, and down my thighs. My knees were starting to buckle, and I realized I might like this.

I did manage to open my eyes and saw Henry and Rick looking at me. Henry was hard as a rock, but Rick stroked himself as he looked at me.

I was moaning in between kisses, but I asked them if I could sit. They helped me down to the blanket.

Benny crawled between my legs, and I spread them wide for him. Terrence's supple lips worked well with mine. I could feel my cat get wetter as he French kissed me. It was hard to keep up with the kiss as Benny's tongue danced in my womanhood. Terrence cupped my face in his hand to keep my head from bobbing.

"I want to come in your mouth," I heard Henry say in his light Spanish accent.

I'd almost forgotten about the guy.

He walked over to me, stroking himself. As Terrence focused on another part of my body, Benny came up for air.

Henry's tip was thick as hell, and it spread my mouth wide. I slurped and slobbered on his sensitive tip before he held my head in place and nutted in my mouth. I swallowed the load and sucked the tip. Henry tried to pull out, but I loved hearing him whimper.

I heard Rick comment on how sexy it was.

Finally, I released Henry, and then Terrence said, "Open your pretty mouth."

Terrence slipped his snake into my mouth, and I couldn't catch a breath as it hit the dangly thing in the back of my throat.

"Good girl," he said, ramming it in multiple times. He held my head until he stopped and held himself still.

My eyes were starting to water before he pulled out.

I struggled to catch my breath and clear my vision, but none of them bothered me as I did so.

When they realized I was okay, they all started kissing different parts of my body. Somebody slipped their finger into my kitty cat, and my senses almost couldn't take all of the touches.

"I'm about to come," I said.

I coached them on what it would take for me to get to the climax first, and before I knew it, I felt my body quake.

Two of the men stopped touching me, but I saw

Henry's fingers working in me. I pushed him away and let my body continue to feel ecstasy.

In the midst of my bliss, I heard Rick curse. I looked over at my boyfriend. His jizz was dribbling from his tip and all over his hand.

I smiled at the sight, but I couldn't stay comfortable for long. I realized all of the men had used that moment to put on condoms.

Henry lay on his back on the blanket, pulled me on top, and started speaking to me in Spanish. I had no clue what he was saying, but it was sexy as hell. He swiftly pulled me down his anaconda. I cursed at the feeling of being stretched. While he thrust himself in me, Benny placed his dick in my mouth. I was thankful the condom didn't taste rubbery.

It was not easy multitasking but all of the men were keeping me busy, Benny in my mouth, Henry in my cat, and Terrence tapping his snake on my ass.

I had slobber all over my face when Benny pulled out, but all of the men stepped away when they heard Henry say he was coming.

His face twisted, and he howled as he came. My thighs were tired, but I bounced on him until he softly pushed me off of him.

I smiled wickedly.

They all cheered me on and told me how great I was doing.

I tried to stand, but my legs were wobbly. Benny and Terrence caught me before I could fall.

"Lay your fine ass back on the floor," Terrence said. "Benny. Fuck her missionary."

I did as I was told. Benny licked my cat a few times and slid his snake in. I watched as Terrence stroked himself to me being fucked.

Benny fucked me hard, and I wasn't mad about it.

My knees were on my chest as he pounded in me, and I squirted. I've only been having sex for a few years. and Rick and Benny were the only ones who've made me squirt. He pulled out and rubbed his dick on my geyser multiple times.

Benny gave me a few more strokes before he pulled out, stood over me, took off the condom, and came over my face.

All the men cheered.

I was too afraid to open my eyes, but I felt a wet cloth on my face. When I did open my eyes, I saw Rick was cleaning me up.

"Are you okay? Do you need a break?" he asked me.

"I'm fine, baby," I said, trying to assure both of us.

"Terrence. Don't be so rough on my girl," he said.

"I'll take care of her," Terrence said. "I'm soft as hell, though," he told me.

He took the condom off and put his dick in my face.

My mouth got his dick as hard as a stone. The veins on him resembled the ridges on a Twix. He put on a fresh condom and told me to get on all fours. I did so, and I felt him enter me slowly.

"Fuck!" I heard him whisper. He rubbed his hands all over my ass and squeezed.

His strokes were slow, and I appreciated it. We picked up the rhythm really well.

Rick came over and kissed my lips passionately.

It was not easy doing that while feeling my cheeks clap against Terrence, but I know it looked good from every angle.

I did a kegel around his snake multiple times.

"I want to come in your pussy so bad," I heard Terrence say through clenched teeth.

Rick sternly said, "Nobody comes in her but me."

I moved my hands behind me and held Terrence's hand as we made clapping noises throughout the living room.

Finally, I heard an animalistic noise come from him, and I was sure he'd blown his load into the condom. I threw my ass back on him some more until he said, "Enough!"

He pulled out.

Rick sat next to me as Terrence collected himself. Rick laid the both of us on our side.

By this point, I was tired. I needed another shower and a rubdown.

"You been taking cock very well tonight," he said.

He used his hand to tap his anaconda at my entrance. I whimpered at the feeling. I didn't know if I would come again, but I was aching for him.

"I can't wait to come in this pussy," he said in my ear as he entered me.

I was a little sore, but for the next five minutes, he took his time making love to me. I felt like he was swimming in me, and my body made waves of pleasure for both of us. He continued to whisper statements in my ear: "You fucking deserve Europe" or "Come on this dick, baby."

Terrence even came back over and rubbed on my clit as Rick worked in me.

"Oh shit!" I exclaimed as I felt my body get bubbly all over, and I burst into waves of quivering. I know I squirted because Terrence talked about it later.

Rick didn't let up, and I continued to feel waves of

pleasure until I heard him say, "I'm coming in you baby. Fuck! I'm fucking coming."

He gave a few more pumps until we both came back to our senses.

I felt like I'd run a marathon or had pulled a studying all-nighter.

Rick pulled out, and I felt the creampie dripping out of me.

He stood up and helped me off the ground. I toppled over from feeling like jelly. He pulled me up again and securely held me as he kissed me.

Benny came down the stairs and said, "I ran her bath like you said, boss. Terrence is in the basement shower. Henry is knocked out. I'm going to the shower."

"Thank you," Rick said.

He picked me up bridal style and took me upstairs. In the bathroom, I saw bathing oil, Epsom salt, and lit candles.

Rick helped me into the tub and said, "Don't worry about anything. I got you."

My body was thankful for the hot water and ingredients in the tub. He washed my hair and helped me bathe.

Diary. That is how I earned a trip to Europe courtesy of Rich Rick.

I Don't Care Who Sees
by Victoria Walsh

"Jenny! We leave in a week. Have you started packing your clothes?" her husband, Keith, yelled from the kitchen of their house.

Jenny popped her head out of the master bedroom and said, "I'm starting now. I know you packed already."

Her husband had just finished dishes and was drying his hands on the hand towel.

Their kids were at a friend's house tonight, and they were thankful.

In a week, Keith and Jenny were going to a swingers resort in the Bahamas for a five-day trip. They didn't need the kids to see what they were packing.

They'd been trying out the swinger lifestyle for the last six months.

It was Jenny's idea.

Keith was excited because they hadn't had any alone time in the last two weeks. He walked into the bedroom, hoping she was packing something sexy for the trip.

Jenny was folding her clothes, and Keith noticed she was including some of the stuff he loved to see her in. There was a cheetah print outfit, two different bathing suits, and two pieces of lingerie.

One of the bathing suits was his favorite—a purple and gold two-piece. Jenny had lost weight a few years ago, and while he did miss her thickness, his wife still had a body he couldn't get enough of. Her bra size H breasts had gone down to a triple-D, and she still had a muffin top. She'd never had an ass before, but now she had one that he loved to smack.

"Remember when we were in Key West last year for our ten-year wedding anniversary?" he asked her.

"Hell yeah!" she said. "Do you remember what we did on the balcony?"

"Of course I do!" Keith smiled because he remembered how it had gone down.

On that trip, they'd stayed at an expensive apartment in Key West. They had just gone for a swim in the pool, and Keith hadn't been able to keep his lips or hands off her. She was so ready for his cock inside her pussy.

They'd taken a shower together in the hotel room, and he'd convinced her to air-dry her hair outside.

"Come here," he told her as they went out to the balcony. She walked into his embrace and asked, "Why?"

"I want you to suck my cock," he told her.

"Baby," she'd protested. "I already didn't want to come out here naked."

"Nobody is watching," he laughed. "And if they are, we'll give them a show. They don't know us personally." He started kissing her ear and whispered, "I want those lips wrapped around my piece tight."

"Babe!" she exclaimed.

"I'll make it worth your while," he told her.

Jenny's supple hands made their way down his flat stomach. She grabbed his cock and firmly pumped it a few times before kissing up and down the seven inches of flesh. Keith quivered when his tip was engulfed in her mouth.

"Damn, your mouth feels like a warm jacuzzi."

Her lips sucked in a few more inches, and she used her hand in a twisting motion as she sucked on his tip. He held on to the balcony rail for balance, and she continued the motion until he pushed her way.

If anyone was watching, they would have seen her head bobbing up and down his cock, making it slipperier than sunscreen.

"I'm going to explode," he moaned, pushing harder into her mouth. She used her hands on the glistening cock.

It wasn't long before she felt his seed spill onto her lips and into her mouth. She sucked harder, and his body began to convulse.

Then they made their way to the bedroom, and he fucked her into paradise.

That night, when they went to dinner at one of the restaurants, a gay male couple pulled Jenny to the side and said, "We saw you working your lips today. You go, girl!"

Jenny and Keith laughed all about it throughout the rest of the trip.

Jenny couldn't help but laugh again now.

"I love how adventurous you've been these last few months," Keith told her.

"I think I want to be more adventurous this trip."

Keith grinned. "I know you will. We're going to a swingers resort with eleven other couples. That's adventurous."

"Well, I know we'll be doing that discreetly in

buildings, but I want more public sex," she told him. "Like maybe sex on the beach."

"Oh shit!" Keith exclaimed. "I don't believe it."

"And I don't care who sees," she said.

Keith liked the sound of that.

* * *

"Bye, Mama. Bye, Dad," their kids said as they kissed their parents goodbye.

Keith and Jenny had their neighbors drop them off at the airport. The kids waved them off from TSA, and the couple left for their vacation. They would fly into Miami and take a cruise ship to the Bahamas.

They met so many interesting people on the cruise. There were two couples that had been swinging with in recent months who were also headed to the resort.

The first couple was Summer and Prince Simpson. The second couple was Tyrone and Amelia Hanes.

* * *

Keith and Jenny arrived at the resort well-rested. They arrived at their villa that would house them and the other two couples for the next five days. It had a wonderful view, a balcony, and a fully stocked kitchen.

On the beds in each room were invitations to the functions the resort was having the next day. There were two events—one pajama-themed and the other sports-themed.

After getting settled in their rooms, they all sat down with drinks to get better acquainted. Summer and Prince said they had been swingers for five years, while Tyrone and Amelia said they'd been doing it for two years. Summer said she had slept with resort staff and a line cook at one of the restaurants not too far from the resort.

Amelia said that she and Tyrone had abstained from sex for the last month so they could have an orgasmic weekend. When the ladies were by themselves that night at dinner, and the men were getting their drinks, she told them she couldn't wait to meet more couples. She said she wanted to have sex with at least three men during the trip.

"Will you keep Keith busy for me?" Jenny asked Amelia.

Amelia gave her a grin. "You know I will."

The three couples didn't live too far from each other back home. While Keith said Summer was fun to be around, he was way more sexually attracted to Amelia.

Jenny understood how. Amelia had olive skin, big eyes, long eyelashes, and—even though it seemed weird to say—a pretty mouth. Her body was shaped like a video vixen's, and Keith couldn't get enough of it.

She knew Amelia was a sexual catch, and she was okay with Keith being with her. Especially since Jenny always found a man that wanted her.

*** * ***

The next morning, Jenny woke to the sun's rays permeating their room. Her body felt well-rested, but she wanted to lie in bed for a while. But she checked the time on her phone and saw that it was 10 a.m. She was shocked.

Usually, when she slept in, it was only until about eight. The kids kept her so busy in the mornings, sleeping past then was a real luxury.

When she awoke, Keith was in the shower, so she joined him. He looked so well-rested, she realized they really had needed this trip.

After showering, he told her he had a picnic planned for them. She put on a red and white sundress. He was going to the beach shirtless in red trunks.

It was breakfast-themed, and he had everything

packed already. They'd brought all the picnic essentials to the beach and ate their light breakfast while watching families playing in the sand or throwing frisbees and women reading under umbrellas. He'd brought wine for them. Jenny usually didn't drink alcohol this early in the morning, but for vacation, she didn't mind.

After eating, they sat on the blanket, her between his legs and him holding her from behind.

"What are you looking forward to for the pajama party?" he asked her.

"Meeting new men. I like the fact that I may never see them again."

"I'm looking for a threesome tonight. I know it's not your style, but I want one. And of course, Amelia."

"She said she is looking forward to being with you this weekend," Jenny told Keith.

"You're only saying that because she keeps me busy. You know I want to be on you all the time."

He started kissing her neck, and she squealed in delight.

Keith pulled back from her and said, "Let's take a walk real quick. Let's leave everything here. The guys will get it."

Out of nowhere, Prince and Tyrone showed up,

greeted her, and gathered the picnic items to take back to the resort.

She knew Keith had something up his sleeve, but she didn't know what.

They walked several miles to a spot on the beach where a small American flag and a blanket were set out under a shade tree.

"What's this?" she inquired.

"Your sex on the beach," he said, helping her to the ground.

"You remembered," she cooed to him.

"I did." He grinned. "Let me help you out of this dress."

She obliged, and he liked what she had on underneath—a white strapless bra holding her triple Ds with matching white panties. He pulled her underwear down to feast on her pussy. He immediately used his tongue and mouth to devour her sensitive flesh. Her moans and the crashing of the beach waves were music to his ears.

It made his cock grow hard.

She loved looking down and seeing his head bob for her. He started fingering her, and she rocked herself on his fingers. She breathed out, "Put your cock in me, Keith."

He pulled his trunks off and kissed her mouth. She

loved that she tasted like the sweet wine they'd had on their picnic. He used his hand to guide his cock into her pussy.

She let out a soft "Fuck" as she reveled in feeling him inside of her.

Keith worked his piece right away as he swiveled his hips to cater to her pussy. It was not long before their cadence was in accord. The breeze added to the ambiance as he continued to rock himself in her and whisper sweet nothings in her ear. He laid her on her side, and while the sand was annoying to both of them, they pushed through it.

She had heard footsteps near them, but she didn't care. She continued to match all of his movements.

The breeze and waves added to her heavy breathing, and she felt a calm cross her as they moved in a smooth motion, whispering their love for each other. She gripped his hand tightly as she felt serenity throughout her body. She closed her eyes as she came to her peaceful climax, and he felt her walls tighten and pulse around him.

He hit his climax and spilled himself in her. He mumbled that he didn't want it to end, and she smiled because she didn't want it to either. But she wanted to explore other things nearby.

He pulled out and crawled on top of her. They kissed wildly, but she warned, "Slow down. We need our energy for the pajama party."

In between soft kisses on her lips, he said, "I don't want to slow down. I want more of you before the party."

She knew she was lying to herself. Exploring the area sounded fun, but she wanted to explore him more.

Jenny told him she wanted to be on top. They switched places, and she rode both of them to their next orgasm. Afterward, they lay content in the sun's rays before cleaning up and heading back to the villa.

* * *

The pajama party was to start at 6 p.m. Presentation mattered to Jenny and Keith. They took separate showers, moisturized their bodies, and made themselves look as attractive as possible.

Jenny thought Keith had the outfit. It was a burgundy and gold satin pajama set. The outline of his dick was visible, and she understood why—he had to advertise to 11 women.

Jenny was wearing a pink mumu. Her lingerie

underneath was a pink lace bodysuit. She curled her hair in large ringlets. The only makeup she was wearing was eyelashes and matte burgundy lip wear.

All three couples headed upstairs to meet the other couples in The Swing Suite. Summer, Amelia, and Jenny gushed over each other's outfit choices. The men carried on with their own shenanigans.

When they arrived in The Swing Suite, there were many men and women socializing. One couple was already making out in a corner.

Keith grabbed her hand and said, "I won't leave until you meet a guy."

She was thankful he didn't go off with Amelia right away and said, "Thank you."

Staff walked around half-naked, carrying trays of wine and glasses. Looking around, Jenny saw a man that caught her eye.

He resembled the actor Chris Evans, and Jenny wanted to caress his beard and take off his pajamas. It looked like all he was wearing was a plush gray robe. Her mind could only imagine what was underneath.

"I think I found the one," she told Keith.

"You're sure?" he asked.

"I'm positive," she said before kissing him.

Jenny walked over to the attractive man and struck

up a conversation with him. As they talked, he couldn't stop looking at her breasts in the mumu. He'd never thought that item of clothing could ever look so good.

His name was James, and he asked her to follow him.

A naked waitress added more wine to Jenny's glass as they walked to one of the rooms in the suite.

The room had minimal decorations and lighting. The soft nighttime sounds added to the pajama party. There was a nice queen-sized bed in the middle with end tables.

"Leave the door open," she said. "I don't care who sees."

She took a final sip of her wine and placed it on an end table. Turning to him, she reached for the belt of his robe, but he held her hands in place.

"Sheez. You're beyond ready, aren't you?"

"Yes," she said. "I learned what I needed to learn about you outside the door. Now let go of me."

James was intrigued and smiled back. "You're full of action. I love it," he said.

She undressed them in between the kisses. He tantalized her nipples and neck with his tongue. Her body was buzzing.

She usually preferred when men ate her out, but she was as wet as a rushing river. His dick was hard enough to make the earth split. She wanted to be earth because she was ready for his length and girth.

Jenny climbed on top of him and positioned him at her entrance. She almost came as his piece penetrated her.

With how tightly their bodies were intertwined and how well they melded together, she knew she would probably come first. Her legs and hips were helping her reach her goal quickly.

"Don't stop," he mumbled as she continued to put the moves on him.

He watched in awe as her eyes rolled to the back of her head as she bounced on his dick.

"Fuck!" she let out as she changed her rhythm.

She worked her hips as if she was working his dick like a stick shift.

Finally, she hit the correct gear and slowed her motions. "I just came."

By this time, there was a small crowd of three at the door.

James placed her on her back and started the strokes he needed to orgasm. Jenny enjoyed being watched by the others.

It helped her be more spontaneous. And she loved them seeing her help James get to climax.

He came inside her, and the others clapped at the show.

James pulled out and kissed her.

"I also don't care who sees," he said.

Three's a Crowd
by Nate Simmons

CALVIN AND HIS WIFE ALISHA MADE THEIR way to one of Atlanta's many sports bars. It was football season, and he wanted to catch a game outside of the house.

He was wearing his Atlanta Falcons gear, while Alisha was in a red and silver skirt and blouse set to show support.

Calvin was there for the wings and liquor. She was just ready for drinks.

The conservative Black couple didn't drink often, but they did social drinking. She got comfortable at the bar as the bartender came over and asked for her order.

Alisha could not get over how attractive he was. He resembled the comedian Matt Rife.

She ordered herself two Disaronnos with a Dr. Pepper.

"That's a smooth drink," he told her. "Most people order something a little sweeter."

"I typically order something sweeter. But I know this will go better with the wings that are served here."

The two smiled at each other.

Meanwhile, Calvin had met a couple of Falcons fans in the back, and they were hitting it off. Alisha was glad because Calvin normally kept to himself. He was a personable man, but he kept his circle small. He didn't have to be an alpha all the time.

Alisha knew she was more outgoing than him. That's how they balanced each other.

She was shocked at how fast her drinks came. There were about a dozen other folks at the bar, and only the Matt Rife-looking bartender and two others were working.

Every so often, Calvin looked back at Alisha to make sure she was comfortable. And she seemed content.

After the first quarter of the game, he was on his way to the bathroom when he saw the bartender talking with his wife.

His face was damn near her ear. He chalked it up to it being loud in there.

Calvin let it slide and handled business. On his way out, he checked on her, and she said, "I'm fine. Mark, the Bartender, is keeping me busy. I'm on drink three, and the wings are filling me up."

"Please keep her occupied," Calvin said. "I don't want her to be bored while I'm enjoying the game."

He kissed her on the cheek and went back to his friends.

All of second quarter, Mark kept visiting and talking to her. He couldn't keep his eyes off her DSL— dick sucking lips. He wanted them on his dick badly.

She had a gorgeous face with round eyes, big lips, and a small mole next to her upper lip.

The bar counter covered the rest of her body, but he imagined she had curves for days. One thing he'd noticed about Atlanta was that most Black women there had amazing curves.

Alisha managed to learn more about him. He was 25 and bartended on the weekends. He was a school-teacher during the week.

She would have loved to see his fine self in class. He could clap her erasers any day. She'd want every tutoring session with him.

Calvin noticed the man looking at his wife's ample breasts. He didn't mind. He couldn't get over how much the bartender was in his wife's ear.

She was eating it up too, because she couldn't stop giggling.

Halftime came around, and the bartender was busy. Alisha didn't mind, though. She paid her tab and went to check on Calvin. He introduced her to the crew of men and women he'd met.

Once the third quarter hit, she sat right back at the bar and enjoyed the attention from Mark. He smelled so good, and she could not stop looking into his blue eyes.

She was thinking inappropriately of his lips. She wanted them on her honey pot.

She assumed it was the liquor talking.

It was mid-third quarter when the bartender said he had to go on break.

Alisha was a little bummed out, but he gestured to her to join him.

Calvin saw the little exchange. His wife texted him she was going outside for fresh air, but he knew she was going to talk to the bartender.

Calvin was done drinking and stumbled to a window to watch the two from the distance.

They looked good together, and she looked alive. Calvin hasn't seen her this alive in several months. Alisha was playing shy, but Calvin knew she wasn't.

Alisha and Mark hugged. He could tell Mark

wanted to rest his hands on Alisha's ass, but Mark stopped himself.

Calvin could not lie. This was turning him on. He could see sparks fly between them, and he wanted to fuel the fire.

When the two came back in at the start of the fourth quarter, Calvin wasn't even thinking about the game.

His dick throbbed at the sight of his wife flirting with another man. Liquid courage was working on him.

He snuck up on them and hugged Alisha from behind. She enjoyed his embrace when he sloppily kissed on her ear.

"You two are having fun over here," he drawled out.

"Oh yes," she said, helping to hold him up.

"You think she's hot, don't you?" Calvin asked Mark.

Mark was embarrassed and did not want to say anything.

"Look at him; he's blushing, baby," Calvin whispered to her. "You want a piece of him, don't you?"

"Baby. Lower your voice."

"I can't help it. He wants you, and I want to see you two flirt some more."

"I need to put more food in you," Alisha said.

"I saw you almost place your hands on her ass," he slurred. "She knows how to throw that peach-shaped ass."

"Calvin!" she exclaimed. "What's gotten into you?"

"The liquor," he cackled loudly. "I want him in you, though."

Mark watched what was unfolding upon him. Calvin wasn't about to harm Alisha, but Mark felt he was about to make an offer.

"This is not like him," she told Mark. Her heart rate was increasing. She was embarrassed.

"I catch that ass when she throws it at me. I sometimes can't handle it."

Mark was going to shoot his shot.

He leaned into the couple and asked, "Are you offering her to me?"

Alisha clutched the imaginary pearls around her neck.

"I can't handle her all by myself. Join us," Calvin slurred.

"Calvin!" she shrieked.

"Unless you don't want me to," Mark said to her. "I don't want to make you uncomfortable."

She cleared her throat and smiled at him. She needed to change the subject.

"We're fine. Nothing is being offered. I'm going to take him to the car. Can you help me?"

Mark assisted her. They put Calvin in the passenger seat as he continued to tell Mark to come to their house.

"Can you give me your number?" Mark asked. "Let me know you made it home safely."

Alisha exchanged numbers, and Mark worried about them getting home safely.

Twenty-five minutes later, he received a text that they'd made it home safe, but she also sent him their address and a text that said, "Come thru."

He smirked.

Calvin knew this was not like Alisha, but he could tell she was interested in Mark, the Bartender. She'd admitted that she had a connection with Mark, and she couldn't figure out how.

The young bartender texted back he would arrive within an hour.

Mark finished work, left work, bought some condoms, and headed to their address.

He was nervous as hell. He had never been in a threesome before. He'd never had sex with someone's wife, either.

The young bartender had never seen a man offer his wife to a stranger before.

He drove to their house and was amazed. It was a small colonial-style home in a nice neighborhood.

He knocked on the door to the quaint home, and Alisha opened it. She smiled upon seeing him and escorted him in.

Once inside, he picked her up and twirled them around. She giggled.

"I see you changed your mind," Calvin's voice said as he watched in the foyer.

Mark put Alisha down and saw Calvin only had a towel wrapped around his waist.

Mark said, "Who could refuse this offer?"

"We've never done this before," Alisha assured Mark. "I didn't want you to think we do this all the time."

"It makes me feel better," he said. "But I need to know what it feels like to be in you."

She smiled and looked at the ground to not get drawn into his eyes.

Calvin grabbed the bag of condoms and spoke up.

"I think you two should go shower," Calvin said. "I'll meet you in the guest bedroom."

Alisha walked Mark to the bathroom.

Alisha could count on one hand the few times she

and Calvin had taken a shower together. And the few times they had, it was not as fun, intimate, and inviting as with Mark.

Mark's eye contact rarely broke during the steamy exchange. He even fingered her until she came. She used soap to write her name on Mark's body.

Alisha learned that Mark was a great kisser. Calvin kissed her only in the morning before work and before bed.

After the shower, Mark dried them both off.

Mark was a grower, not a shower. And she was okay with that.

They couldn't keep their hands off each other as they walked into the guest bedroom naked.

Calvin was lying on his back in the bed. Alisha was shocked that his dick was already hard. The last few months it had been hard to keep him up. She always thought he was too young for that, but today it was the last thing on her mind.

Mark could care less about seeing the married man stiff.

Alisha crawled on the bed and started sucking on Calvin's dick. Mark was intrigued watching a naked Alisha slurp on it like it was a popsicle.

He knew her mouth knew how to suck dick.

Calvin smacked her Georgia peach in the process. His grunts were more animalistic.

Mark's dick was getting harder, seeing her mouth move on her husband. He started stroking himself at the sight.

"Good girl," Calvin said to Alisha, rubbing on her back.

"Don't just stand there with your dick in your hand. Come get some," Calvin called out to Mark.

Mark got on the bed and forced Alisha's mouth off Calvin, and placed her head in the direction of his dick.

Calvin and Mark probably didn't know Alisha was a little nervous about having two men share her body, but she was going to handle it like a good girl.

Mark let out a "fuck" when her mouth met his dick.

Calvin loved seeing his wife in action. She was handling all of Mark's length and girth.

"I want you to fuck me while he's in your mouth," Calvin told his wife.

Calvin grabbed lubricant for her honeypot.

"Get on all fours," he told his wife. She did, not missing a beat with Mark. Calvin gripped her Georgia peach before sliding his dick into her honeypot.

"Shit!" she said, letting Mark fall from her mouth.

She stroked Mark's dick while Calvin gave her slow, sweet strokes.

Calvin talked rough, nasty shit to her as he continued to pick up his pace and fuck her harder.

Mark kissed her lips before putting his dick back in her mouth.

Calvin relished calling her a good girl and seeing her handle both him and Mark.

Before she knew it, Calvin was telling her he was going to come. She stopped working on Mark and made sure her strokes matched Calvin's thrusts. He loved seeing her peach clap as she did this.

He came inside of her, and she didn't stop.

Calvin's grunts were more animalistic due to her actions. He felt pleasure, relief, and joy all in those 30 seconds of his orgasm.

Calvin pulled out and walked to the guest bathroom as he caught his bearing.

Alisha grabbed a condom and passed it to Mark, who put it on himself. The young man lay on the bed, and Alisha got on top of him. He quickly used his lips to attack hers. She skillfully grabbed his dick and placed him in her honeypot amid the kiss.

"Fuck," they whimpered in unison.

Mark watched as she buried her face in his chest as

he massaged her honeypot with his dick. His strokes were soft and purposeful.

Mark felt like her honeypot was a sticky warm spot just for him and Calvin.

"Look at me, please," he murmured.

The pleasure was so good. She didn't know how to open her eyes and focus on him.

When she finally did, he still gave her soft strokes. She felt like she was going to melt under his gaze.

Her breathing was starting to come closer together. He sped up his strokes and said, "Focus on me."

She wanted to say words, but the only thing that came out was her quick breathing. She knew her orgasm was approaching.

"Don't hold it in," he said.

She clenched herself around his dick to come faster. The slushing sound of her honeypot permeated the room. Their bodies made clapping noises as she came closer to her climax.

Mark always heard slow and steady wins the race, but seeing it in action was breathtaking.

A screech escaped her lips as she reached the finish line. Mark continued working his dick as she finally closed her eyes. She leaned in to kiss him, and they were forehead to forehead as he slowed his strokes.

Her breathing was so heavy, and her face was so

calm. He smiled, knowing he'd given her a piece of peace.

"You two look great together," Calvin said.

Mark had forgotten Calvin existed. That intimate moment was beautiful, and he didn't need Calvin coming to ruin it. He rolled his eyes and held on to Alisha a little longer.

"I'm tired," she told them as she lifted herself off of Mark.

Calvin wanted more action with the three of them, but he said, "Whatever you want to do, we'll do."

"I would like for Mark to stay the night, but I'm sure he works tomorrow."

Mark got out of the bed and said to her, "I'll do a half day tomorrow. I want to spend the rest of the night with you."

Calvin asked Mark to escort Alisha to the shower. As Mark did so, Calvin pulled the bedding off and placed it on a wash cycle. He pulled a fresh set of bedding out of the closet and remade the bed.

Afterward, he went to go shower.

By the time he finished his night routine and placed the bedding in the dryer, Alisha and Mark were curled up in the guest bedroom bed.

Calvin stayed on the edge of the bed, Alisha in the middle, and Mark on the other side of her.

It wasn't long before morning came, and Calvin's work alarm went off. It was 7:30 a.m., and Alisha wasn't curled up with Mark. She was curled up with Calvin.

Calvin didn't need an ego boost often, but that did something to his ego.

He turned off all the other alarms on his phone and looked at his beautiful wife.

Her skin was glowing, her mouth was slightly parted, and her lips were pouted. He gave her a quick kiss on her cheek and fell asleep.

Calvin woke up an hour later to the sounds of soft giggling and smooching noises.

"You're hard as a rock," he heard Alisha mumble to Mark.

"My morning wood," Mark said in between kisses.

Calvin rolled over and saw Alisha on her side, talking to Mark. He snaked his arm over her side.

Alisha pulled away from Mark and said, "Morning, baby," to Calvin.

"Morning," he said, snuggling close to her so she could feel his morning wood on her Georgia peach.

Alisha chirped, "You both have enough wood for me, I see."

"Damn right," Calvin said.

He used the hand closest to her chest to knead her breasts through her nightshirt.

Alisha was really moaning through Mark's kisses now.

Calvin removed himself from her and said, "Mark, hold up."

Mark didn't want to stop, but he did as he was told.

Alisha and Mark watched as Calvin pulled her nighttime shorts off her and started to give her head.

Alisha let out a soft gasp as his tongue worked on her. Mark took this as his cue to focus on her.

He helped her out of her shirt and started sucking on her nipples.

Alisha enjoyed having one man on her nipples and the other in her pussy. The pleasure felt so good she thought she was going to cry.

Calvin didn't let up; he used skills on her he hadn't used in a while. Her body was responding well to both of them.

Mark stroked himself as he saw Alisha grip the sheets tighter.

He wanted her to come, but only while he was inside of her. He asked for a condom, and Calvin stopped what he was doing to pass him one. Calvin kissed his wife on the lips as Mark slipped into her slippery honeypot.

She gripped the bedsheets tighter and kissed Calvin harder. It made his dick harder. He needed to be inside of her somehow. He helped her lift up her upper body and slid the tip of his dick in. He just needed it a little wet. He pulled out and stroked himself.

Mark was still working her honeypot, and he told her, "I'm coming."

Calvin watched as Alisha told Mark not to stop. Mark pounded faster in her pussy as she talked him into his orgasm.

He let out a "Fuck" and a final thrust as he felt his seed spill into the condom. He didn't want to leave her warmth, but he pulled out and headed to the bathroom.

When he came back, he saw Calvin and Alisha on their side and Calvin putting lubricant on his dick. Alisha was begging him to put himself in her ass.

It had been months since they'd done anal, but she missed it.

Mark watched as Calvin slid his length in between her ass cheeks. It looked like he was putting a hot dog in a bun. He continued to make the motion until he tapped his tip on her asshole.

By this time, Alisha was writhing for the dick and told Calvin to give it to her now.

"Fuck you're so tight," he said upon entering his wife.

Mark had never seen something like this in live-action before. It was thrilling to watch such a beautiful woman take this sexual position with grace. He grabbed another condom, placed it on, and slapped his tip on her clitoris.

The stimulation made her call out both of their names. Both men liked the sound of that. Mark continued to slide his tip over her clitoris several times. She released the grip she had on the sheets as an orgasm washed over her body.

"That's right," Calvin said. "Keep coming."

Alisha let the feeling continue all over her and heard Calvin grunt as he came in her ass. He continued to pump while Mark slipped his dick into her honeypot and felt her body quake.

She looked sexy as hell with her love face. He didn't want it to end. She tried pushing them both away.

Calvin did pull out, but Mark wouldn't give up.

"Fuck, Mark!" she exclaimed as he continued to work on her.

He leaned down and kissed her as he slowly stroked her pussy.

Mark wanted to come again, but for the next seven minutes, he talked and kissed her into her next orgasm. Tears of happiness rolled down her face as she came on Mark's dick once again.

Both men left her to go clean themselves. When they came back, she was lying on her stomach crooked. Her body was spent. She wanted to go back to sleep.

Calvin came back, slapped her Georgia peach, and said, "Let me get you ready for the day."

"Calvin. Just lay with me. I wanna be in your arms."

"Let me get you cleaned up and some food in you," he said. "Once I get you hydrated, you have me for the rest of the day."

As they walked into the bathroom, Alisha told Calvin, "No more sex partners. Three's a crowd. From now, I just want you, me, and Mark."

Calvin gave a smile and said, "Just the three of us."

Dominated

by Kirk Walsh

"Have a great evening, Mr. Wilson," my staff said as we left my dermatology practice.

"You too, ladies," I said as I parted ways with them.

I walked to my Volvo and drove to my favorite diner. I had heard folks talk about me over the years. They wonder why I even come to this diner when I make $300,000 a year.

This diner always gets a visit from me because even though they have about a dozen meals on the menu, there are only three that I love to get. Those are their tender pot roast, shrimp and grits, or country-fried steak.

When I enter, I am greeted by my favorite waitress, Mrs. Simpson. She's been working there for the last 30 years. Then I'm greeted by one of the cooks, Mr.

Thomas. He's been working there for 15 years, and he puts his twist on all the meals.

Mrs. Simpson takes my order, and then she talks to some of the other regulars. I enjoy my meal in peace. I use about fifteen minutes to discuss stocks with Mr. Thomas. I've been using the last three years to educate him on it. I want him to have a decent retirement when he gets older.

I leave $25 tips each for Mrs. Simpson and Mr. Thomas.

Instead of heading to my car, I walk down to the cigar club near my luxury townhouse. I've had the same routine since before my divorce. The diner, the cigar club, and then home.

My ex-wife and I divorced about two years ago. Here I am now, 41 and living good. I'm sure she's living life too. I give her $2,500 a month even though we don't have kids. Because I provided her with a certain lifestyle during our ten years together, I have to pay for that.

I am a block away from the cigar club, and I instantly hear the jazz pouring out the doors. I smile because I know this will be another relaxing evening before heading home.

I enter the establishment and find myself a corner where I can still enjoy the music and stay to myself.

The waitresses are all wearing cheetah dresses tonight. The waiters are in their usual black and white attire.

I never would have noticed something like clothes, but the few times I brought my ex-wife here, she brought it to my attention. The waiters and waitresses only wear about three outfits year-round.

A waitress comes over in her cheetah number. She is a slender woman who has waited on me before. If I weren't opposed to dating, I would have asked her out before.

"How are you tonight, sir?" she inquires.

"I'm doing well this evening," I tell her.

"Do you want your usual, a Padron 1964 Maduro and two Manhattans?"

"Yes. But I want my Manhattans separately."

"Sure thing," she states.

"Thank you, Shelly," I say, looking at her name tag.

She smiles at me, and within minutes I get my Padron and my first Manhattan.

As I puff away on my cigar, I see a regular walk by. We have small talk, and I congratulate him as he tells me sold five houses this week. I applaud him because I remember when he first started in real estate.

He departs when the pretty young thing on his arm says she's ready for a drink to celebrate.

I chuckle once they leave my presence. I don't know if dating is worth it for me. Maybe it's because I'm terrible at compromising. That was one of the things that ruined my marriage.

I'm very set in my ways. I want everything the way I like it, and that's all there is to it.

For the next ten minutes, I enjoy the music, and I'm halfway through my cigar.

Shelly arrives with my final Manhattan.

"Thank you," I say, waving her off.

She comes around with my bill a few minutes after I finish the cigar. She thanks me for the $25 tip I give her. I leave the cigar club and walk back to the diner to get to my car.

* * *

The next day, I start my routine as usual. I do a walk around the neighborhood, eat a light breakfast, masturbate, shower, and head to my practice.

I'm usually a cold person, but sometimes my staff manages to make me smile. They make meeting with 12 patients a day easy.

After the day is over, I head to the diner and enjoy a meal of country-fried steak with mashed potatoes and gravy. My vegetable of choice is green beans.

My usual routine continues as I walk from the diner to the club. Tonight, the music is more bluesy. I'm not mad at it.

The music is tasteful and refreshing as I grab a seat at the bar. This time, Shelly isn't my waitress, but I notice that tonight's cheetah is the dresscode again.

Shelly manages to check in on me occasionally. I don't know why; I'm not her customer tonight.

I try not to talk to her too much because I want a little peace of mind as the blues seeps into my ears and throughout my body.

I applaud her, though. She is beautiful and flirty, even if I am cold and aloof.

While in the middle of my cigar and waiting on my next Manhattan, she comes and talks to me.

"Sir. Why do you never have a date with you? You used to occasionally come with a woman."

"That was my ex-wife," I tell her.

"I'm sorry to hear that," she says. "You're an attractive man. Your milky skin always looks good. Your bald head keeps a nice shine. I can tell you're fit. I would imagine women would be all over you all the time."

"Let me be blunt with you," I said. "Most women won't follow my rules, and I'm sick of compromise."

"Rules?" she inquires.

Tonight I don't feel like explaining myself to

anybody, but since she is being an Inquisitive Izzy, I figure I'll answer her question.

In an effort to cease her questions, I tell her, "When a woman is in my presence, I demand full submission."

"What if she is independent?"

"I love an independent woman, but when it comes to fucking or making love, I expect her to submit to me."

"You're domineering," she says, looking me up and down. "That's interesting."

Before I can ask her what she means, she leaves and tends to other patrons.

I'm a little shocked about our interaction, but she's piqued my interest.

I receive my next Manhattan. Within 15 minutes, I'm walking back to my car.

As I get closer to my car at the diner, I hear someone calling out for me.

"Sir! Sir!" a woman's voice calls.

I stop in my tracks and turn to see Shelly running toward me. She almost trips on her way.

"Did I leave something behind?" I ask her as she stands in front of me, catching her breath.

"I want to finish our interesting conversation

about a submissive woman. I think I can be what you want."

I roll my eyes and tell her, "You seem a little too amorous for me. As soon as my dick is hard, I need a woman to follow all of my orders."

"You've seen me at my workplace," she points out. "I take orders well."

I give her a sly smile for her cleverness.

"The woman I require needs to serve me. She needs to do as she's told—sexually—until I tell her to stop."

"I've been serving you for a few years, haven't I?"

Is my dick starting to stiffen with every remark?

A"nd when I cum, she needs to thank me for fucking her," I tell her.

Shelly grabs my dick through my slacks and gets close to me. I notice a scent of vanilla on her skin as she says, "Let's go to your place, sir. I'll take every order you give me."

I let out a small growl. It's been six months since I've allowed a woman to enjoy my dick. It's been six months since a woman submitted to me.

They all wanted a romantic boyfriend, and I just wanted a good fuck.

"Follow me. I don't live too far from this diner," I tell her.

She releases me and says, "Yes sir."

We travel in different cars to my luxury townhouse.

My mind is going 100 miles a minute as I think of the different ways I can dominate her. My cock is ready to be inside of a woman.

When we arrive at the townhouse, she is mesmerized by it. Most people are. I have eclectic pieces of art, and I keep my furniture to a minimum.

She places her purse on one of my side tables.

I walked her to my sofa so we could start this submission process.

"Take your clothes off for me," I told her. "Give me a show."

The many times I've seen this woman, and I've never actually paid attention to her.

Her tan skin looks great in that cheetah dress. She is a slender woman who looks good in clothes, so I can only imagine how she would look naked. Her blond hair is bone-straight and frames her face perfectly. Her pink lips have a nice gloss on them. I want to kiss it off.

The woman caresses herself slowly, and I remove my pants and underwear. She has a look of shock when she sees my cock spring free. She bites her bottom lip as she lets her dress cascade off her shoulders. Once her dress hits her hips, she shimmies herself out of it. It pools around her ankles, and she steps away from the cheetah-print fabric.

Now she is only wearing a bra and panties. They were mismatched. Poor thing, probably didn't know she was going to get charismatic cock tonight.

"Sir. I didn't know you were so big," she says in a coy tone.

"Call me William or Mr. Wilson," I tell her.

I grip my cock as she calls me William. She takes off her undergarments and lets them fall to the ground. Her breasts are on the smaller side, but her nipples are already erect.

Her garden is nicely groomed, and I toss around in my head if I will feast on it later.

Her hands rub on her ass cheeks, and she squeezes them. It isn't the biggest ass, but it fits her frame, and I want to hold it.

"Come suck this cock," I tell her. She crawls onto the sofa and makes eye contact with my cock like she has an interview with it. I am hoping she is ready for these nine inches.

Her small hand manages to wrap around my girth, and she gladly immerses my cock in her mouth. Saliva drips from her lips as she lets me hit the back of her throat. Her hands twist on my cock, making me close my eyes in pleasure.

"Move your hands," I say. She does as she is told, and I grip her hair into a ponytail as I thrust myself into her mouth.

"You have my cock so slippery and shiny," I say in between her swallowing me. I pull out, and the saliva stretches from her lips to various parts of my cock.

I must say it feels like I am being worshipped. The mouth and the tongue are the wettest softest parts of a person. All I do is lie back and enjoy it. She puts pressure on my cock with her hand. How damn warm and wet she is. I tell her not to let up because I am going to come all over her face.

"Give me all that, Mr. Wilson," she says as she sucks only the tip and strokes the rest of me.

Oh shit! I need to hold on to something because I am going to spill my seed on her face.

My breathing increases as she uses the same lip and hand combo. I let out a quick grunt as my nut flies on her nose, cheeks, and lips.

"Yes, William! Come on my face," she says as I try to catch my breath. I hold on to the sofa for balance as I come off my high.

The woman is stuffing my seed in her mouth, and it makes me want her more.

I run to the kitchen to get her damp paper towels to clean her face.

"My God." I kiss her lips. "I haven't come like that in a long time," I tell her.

She gets off the sofa to dispose of the paper towels.

"Shelly. Bend yourself over the arm of the chair."

Without hesitation, the blonde does as she's told. She even gives me the perfect arch to enter her. I smack her ass and tell her she is behaving very well.

"I need to reward you later," I tell her.

I squat to the ground and start eating her garden from the back.

"Oh God," she says from the contact. She spreads her legs wider for me, and I have so much access to tend to her womanhood.

She is riding my face. I haven't done something like this since my wife.

It is exhilarating hearing her work to ride me and her soft pants. I felt my cock getting hard again, and I stroke myself before sliding myself between her cheeks.

Her garden is pulsing and begging for me. I slide my length into her womanhood, and she stretches wide to receive me.

"Fuck!" she breathes. I don't even move right away as I hear her continue with, "Oh my God."

I watch as I moved in and out of her. She takes more of me with every thrust. I pull out because I felt like I am going to come.

I guess I am still sensitive.

My cock re-enters her, and she says, "Yes, William. Please give it to me."

If I knew she was a sexual beggar, I would have brought her home months ago. I use the next few minutes to let my cock swim in her.

"My legs are throbbing," she tells me.

"I know you got this, baby. You're not tired. I'm almost there."

If the townhouse could talk, it would probably talk about how well she was in rhythm with me. It would talk about how loud we were and didn't care. If it could talk, it would talk about how I pulled out and ordered her to look at me as I turned her around and came on her breasts.

The next thing I know, she's thanking me for giving her more cum.

"Shelly. You keep talking like this and I will fuck you into the morning."

In a quick remark, she says, "I see you, Energizer Bunny. I'm not complaining."

This woman is going to make me come a third time.

"Lie on your back!" I command her.

I tell her to suck my cock again. I have noticed over the years that women do not like to give head while lying down, but my goodness, she opens her mouth wide like a muppet! Her saliva coats me.

I just need it a little wet. I pull out and I am harder than a Jolly Rancher.

I rub myself between her folds and on her clitoris. She elicits the moans I wanted to hear.

Her legs spread wide, and I slide myself inside her. I know I probably shouldn't, but I do fast strokes first.

"Fuck me just like that, Mr. Wilson," she says.

My eyes roll to the back of my head hearing her talk to me like that. I pump in her faster and harder, and she starts squirting on my cock.

I pull out, look at the mess she's created on my sofa, and smile.

"Damn!" I exclaim, tapping myself in her juices.

I slip myself back inside her garden. She feels like a lake. I give her passionate strokes as I kiss different spots on her face. We have a connection that I did not expect. We are unified in our movements, pants, and rhythm. She makes me feel like I could be inside her forever and she wouldn't mind.

My face is buried in the crook of her neck and she has her arms wrapped around me tightly when she comes on me.

Her warm and sticky garden pulsates around me, and I know not to let up. It's her first time coming tonight, and I am pleased with myself for bringing her to the moment.

"Can I come in you, Shelly?" I manage to inquire.

"Please," she says to me.

That's all I need to hear. I stroke in her harder for a few more minutes and release myself inside her garden.

We don't even move as a wave of relief hits me. We are sweating and sticking to each other, and I don't mind.

She is underneath me, saying she wants more.

I can't believe it.

We did three rounds in like 20 minutes, and she wants more?

I pull out, look down at our mess, and smile. Then I look at her. "Good girl. Now what are you supposed to say to me?"

"Thank you for giving me a good fuck. Dominate me some more."

That was exactly what I wanted to hear.

"I demand you take a break," she says.

I burst out laughing and help her off the sofa before getting us both some Gatorade.

I need electrolytes now.

"Thank you, William," she says. "How did I do?"

"I love how you submit to me. I would have

brought you home weeks ago if I knew you could take cock and instruction so well."

She starts blushing.

"I told you I could handle you," she says. "If you asked me to cook you dinner and fuck you afterward, I would do it with no hesitation."

Once again, she has my cock ready to rise.

"Where do you want me to dominate you next?"

"In the shower," she says.

I take her upstairs to the shower, and I am the Energizer Bunny for the next two hours as she submits to me.

The Masseuse
by Megumi Castro

JANINE SAT ON THE AIRPLANE NEXT TO A sleeping baby and its mother. This was a peaceful flight to Hawaii, but she was skeptical about the trip.

It was December, and she was supposed to have a husband with her on this flight, but instead, there she was—single.

Janine was supposed to get married in June and enjoy this trip to Hawaii with her soulmate Pete. But Pete dumped her a month before their wedding. His excuse was lame; he said he didn't feel financially secure to marry her. Her family was a little more well-off and could be financially intimidating, but she told him that his finances were something that could be easily fixed.

He didn't want to hear it.

She refused to let this prepaid Hawaiian honeymoon go to waste. Now here she was, heading to Hawaii. After all, the room at the resort was nonrefundable.

The hospitality as soon as she and the others got off the plane was magnificent. The entertainment and decoration made her feel welcome.

The resort was nice, but when she got to her room, she wished she hadn't come alone.

Jetlag was getting to her, so she took a nap. After the nap, she freshened up and headed out for dinner.

The next morning, she looked at the itinerary for her day-one activities. She was looking forward to getting a massage, and afterward, she was going to use the resort's jacuzzi and pool.

The male masseuse who worked on her made the experience so good. She was going back in a few days.

That night she took herself to a nice dinner at one of the restaurants in the area. She had researched it about a month ago.

The meat was very well seasoned and savory, and the atmosphere was enjoyable.

On day two of the trip, she went snorkeling and

enjoyed nature. By that evening, she noticed she had a slight tan, but she was getting lonely. She had seen a group of friends enjoying the trip, as well as a few happy couples.

She had even met a couple that was there for their honeymoon. She knew that should have been her.

While she was glad Pete wasn't with her, she wished she had some companionship on this trip. Everyone she'd asked to join her had turned her down.

Janine finished all of her activities and grabbed lunch outside in her bikini. She had lost weight since Pete dumped her, but she still managed to look good in her clothes. Her ass looked perfect in the polka-dot bikini bottoms. Her breasts were small, but they sat high in the top.

The sun felt good on her skin, and she was glad she'd put sunscreen on before drying in the sun. Her meal was once again delicious. This was going to be a nice lunch spot for her.

After lunch, she went back to the resort and had a nice nap after her shower. Before she knew it, it was time to head out on a sunset cruise to one of the islands. She met a group of women who planned this girls' trip about eight months ago.

While she did not spend the whole sunset cruise with them, they were warm and comforting. She was glad they'd accepted her into their group. They even started following each other on Instagram.

After the cruise, she went to the bar at the resort and watched a basketball game. It was one of the sports she had watched with Pete. She enjoyed the game while she sipped on fruity drinks.

Once the game ended, she headed upstairs to go to sleep.

The next morning marked day three of the trip. She didn't even do her morning activity. It was one that she and Pete had picked out that was fun to do as a couple. She decided to go to the resort's bar instead.

Janine dressed herself in a purple bathing suit today.

The special was margaritas, so she ordered three.

Janine was chatting with different guests at the bar. The first was a man that told her he had been stationed in Hawaii about a decade ago.

He was so damn attractive! He said he'd come back to visit and decided that he wanted to retire there.

The man looked ageless. He said he was 46, but he didn't look a day over 30.

They were conversing about the island when a local chimed in. She was a pretty woman.

Janine and the man were mesmerized by her looks.

Of all the local women out there, she was one of the thicker ones Janine had met since arriving. The woman was wearing a floral scrub set. Her sleeves showed off the tattoos on her left arm. Her natural eyelashes were thick, her lipstick was dark, and her wavy hair was jet black. Janine wished she had the woman's breasts. They were like coconuts stuffed into medical scrubs.

The attractive woman told them interesting things about the area.

When the man left, Janine ordered her fourth margarita and continued conversing with the local.

"My name is Maile," she told Janine.

"Nice to meet you, Maile," Janine said to her. "I'm Janine."

Janine joked that she was four margaritas in, and Maile was two margaritas behind her. "Are you here to blow off steam too?"

"Hell yeah," the woman said, running her hands through her wavy hair. "I just had an interview to be a massage therapist at the resort," she added. "Once I get the job, I won't be able to use the hotel facilities— guests only!"

"Oh wow! I'm shocked," Janine said. "They have amenities that I see guests aren't utilizing. They might as well let their staff use it."

Maile took a sip of her margarita and said, "Once I get the job, I'll explain the benefits of having staff's usage of amenities."

"You sound like an activist. A leader almost," she said, admiring Maile.

"I can be that way sometimes," she said. "But enough about me. Why are you blowing off steam?"

"This is supposed to be my honeymoon trip."

"Oh shit," Maile said, leaning in to listen.

"But since my ex called off the wedding, I decided to enjoy the trip by myself." Janine grabbed her phone to show Maile how she had been keeping herself busy.

"I guess it's a good thing that man is out of my life," Janine said.

"His loss. You seem like a great woman," Maile said.

"Thanks, girl," Janine said to her, finishing the last of her margarita.

Maile could not stop peeking at Janine's face.

The talk got deeper when Maile began telling Janine that she had recently been dumped by her girlfriend.

"Well, look at that," Janine said. "She just couldn't

handle you, Maile. You seem to be a person interested in healthy relationships. Based on why she broke up with you, she is toxic."

"That she was," Maile agreed.

While she did look at her drink occasionally, she could not keep her eyes off Janine.

Janine was what her ancestors would have called scrawny or skinny. While Janine was certainly slender, her features fit her frame. Her breasts might have been small, but Maile wanted to fit one in her mouth. She wanted to leave hickeys on Janine's neck and run her fingers through her red curly hair.

Her tanned skin really popped in that purple.

And she wanted to spread Janine's legs wide and feast on her womanhood.

She didn't think Janine was into women, but she knew she needed to shoot her shot.

"After hearing what you've been going through, I suggest I give you a massage."

"I definitely need one. I had a great one the other day at the resort."

"My hands work better," Maile said. "Besides, you know you'd rather have a massage than another margarita."

Sensing that Maile was attempting to pick her up,

Janine decided she should make it clear that she wasn't gay.

"I'm into penis, not pussy," she said.

Maile replied, "You don't have to be gay. I can still make you come harder than you've ever come in your life."

Maile smiled as Janine's face flushed pink.

"Don't be embarrassed. I don't bite."

"Maybe I want you to bite," Janine said. "And that's not the drinks talking either."

"I'm glad you said that because I believe in consent."

In a moment of weakness, Janine invited Maile up to her room.

"You won't regret it," Maile told her. She grabbed her massage oils and followed her up to the honeymoon suite.

When they arrived, they found the perfect spot for the massage and sanitized the area. Janine lay on her stomach, and Maile wanted to smack Janine's apple-shaped ass.

"I'm going to loosen your top," she told Janine.

Janine mumbled, "Okay."

Maile's hands were nice and warm as she undid the top, giving her access to Janine's back. The massage started at her neck before her hands started working on Janine's shoulders.

The occasional moans slipped from Janine's mouth, and Maile knew she was doing a good job.

For the next fifteen minutes, her hands worked on Janine's back. Making liberal use of the massage oil, Maile gave her a sensual massage that drew her in like a moth to a flame.

Janine was starting to feel like a new person. She didn't even realize she had spots that needed attention. "Can you get my glutes too?"

"Hell yeah," Maile said in a soothing voice.

One thing she knew was that too much talking could ruin a great massage.

She slipped Janine's bathing suit bottom off and gently catered to Janine's glutes. Her ass cheeks were so big, she needed both hands on one cheek.

Janine didn't want to admit it, but her womanhood was throbbing. She'd felt the same way when the man had given her a massage a few days before.

"I'm almost done," Maile said, working her hands back to the top of Janine's body.

"No," she said. "It feels good, I don't want it to stop."

"Do you want a happy ending?"

Janine looked up and said, "How did you know I needed one?"

"I didn't," she said. "Your body is responding to me well, and I don't want to stop touching you."

Maile's fingers worked like an itsy-bitsy spider as they moved back to her ass. Maile massaged the ass cheeks and told Janine, "Spread your legs a little wider."

Janine did as she was told, and Maile slipped a finger inside of her from the back.

Maile whispered, "You're wetter than the island."

Janine couldn't speak; it just felt good to have someone else inside of her, other than herself.

Maile's hands and fingers collaborated to give Janine a happy ending. The sloshing noises were the perfect sounds for the occasion. Janine rocked herself on Maile's finger and said, "I'm going to come on your fingers."

"Wait!" Maile said, pulling out.

Janine wanted to cuss her out.

"I want to see your face when you cum," Maile explained.

Janine wasted no time in flipping herself over. She was now on her back and spreading her legs to give Maile access to her.

Maile knew how to work her fingers inside of

Janine's womanhood and how to put the right amount of pressure on her clit.

Janine started rubbing on her own titties and twisting her nipples as she got closer to her happy ending.

She clenched her walls around Maile's fingers and fondled herself some more as she came.

"Yes, baby girl," Maile said. "Just like that. Keep cumming for me." She didn't let up on sending more shocks of pleasure through Janine's body. Janine started closing her legs, and Maile withdrew her fingers and watched as Janine lay there with her body enjoying the aftermath.

When Janine finally came back to reality thirty seconds later, Maile was washing her hands at the sink. Janine lifted up her body, noticing that her titties were exposed.

Maile bit her bottom lip at the sight.

"Take off your clothes and meet me on the bed," Janine told Maile.

Maile didn't even hesitate.

When she finished undressing, Janine was watching her. Janine finally paid attention to the beauty in front of her. Maile had to be at least 5' 10", towering over Janine's 5'3". Her titties were massive, her stomach was flat, and she had wide hips and a bubble butt. Her skin was a bit darker than Janine's.

Maile's eyes were the perfect almond shape and light brown. Janine wanted to stare at her all day.

Her wavy hair framed her face perfectly.

As Maile crawled onto the bed, she saw that Janine was pulling a dildo out of her suitcase.

"I can help you with that," she told the slender woman.

"I'm not using it yet."

Janine told Maile that while she did just have a good orgasm, she hadn't come hard.

"It's been seven months since someone touched me like that. But I expect you to make me come harder."

"I'll do just that," Maile said.

Janine leaned into Maile and started kissing her dark lips.

Maile couldn't believe how great of a kisser Janine was. They could barely keep their hands off each other. Janine's body was still slippery from the oil, and Maile felt it added to their experience. She watched as Janine pursed her lips to suck on her sensitive nipples.

She moaned at the attention to her titties, getting wetter by the second. She returned the favor to Janine and started kissing down her body.

Her body was crazy sensitive; everything felt good —each nip, tug, or kiss on her skin ignited her body and moistened her womanhood.

Her mouth quivered at the feeling of Maile kissing her thighs. Everything was tender, sweet, and sensual. Their giggles, kisses, and light breathing bounced off the walls in the suite.

This is how she'd imagined her honeymoon to be: hot, sticky, and wet. She imagined multiple orgasms while being sweaty and sexy. Maile had already provided her one orgasm, and she wanted one more.

Maile glided her tongue on Janine's pussy folds. Her tongue did all the work by assaulting Janine's sensitive flesh. Janine's knees were in her chest as Maile worked on her, and she felt like she was going to cry from the pleasure.

Janine was fueling Maile's ego with all the moaning she was doing. She fingered herself before putting her lips on Janine's clit.

Janine started moaning, gasping louder. Maile didn't stop sucking; instead, she inserted her fingers into the tanned beauty. Janine moaned wildly, telling Maile not to stop.

She felt herself about to come, and Maile switched between her fingerplay and tending to Janine's womanhood and clit.

"Focus on the clit," Janine managed to whisper out.

Maile did just that and watched as Janine played with her titties and came on Maile's tongue. Maile continued to use her mouth and fingers on Janine. Janine's body shook as she squealed from her climax.

Maile came up for air and continued to finger the beauty beneath her. She told her to ride her wave.

Janine then squirted on Maile. Maile sucked it up like a vacuum and then started kissing on Janine's breasts and nipples.

"If the resort doesn't hire you," Janine said in between breaths, "I'll get a massage from you every day that I'm here."

"You came so hard on me," Maile said. "I told you I could do it."

"You are my favorite masseuse," Janine said in between kissing Maile. "I'll come hard on you any day."

"Now pass me that dildo so I can use it to massage your pussy," Maile said.

Janine grinned big. This was the companionship she needed.

Who knew her trip would perk up because of a masseuse?

Caged
by Simon G.

"WHERE'S THE KEY?" I ASKED MY DOM, Vanessa, as she settled into my apartment.

"As your keyholder, I'm not telling you where I have it," she said.

I led her to the sofa and said, "I'm so fucking anxious. I am ready to be released from the cage."

I'd been wearing a cock cage for seven days. I know I'm going to nut so much tonight.

A cock cage is literally a cage that goes over a man's flaccid penis, fastened with a lock and key, which prevents him from getting hard.

"I don't know. I liked seeing you beg this week," she said as she settled on the sofa next to me.

I've been wearing this cage for seven days because I arrived on our last date ten minutes late.

I can admit, I was late for a frivolous reason—I was too busy masturbating.

At first, I found the cage sexy. As the days went on, it was cruel behavior. Now I'm ready to plunge myself in her. I don't care if it is in her mouth, vagina, or ass.

Vanessa told me she was so turned on knowing the key around her neck was the only way I could find some relief. Today it wasn't around her neck, and I wanted to know where she'd put it.

For the last seven days, she would kiss me, caress me, whisper the dirtiest, sexiest shit in my ear, and I just couldn't get hard. The only time she removed the cage from me was when I had to pee. On my third night, it was painful to sleep with it.

So she took it off me. You would think I would be a sneak and masturbate, but I didn't. I was too tired from working my job and being chaste.

Out of the seven days, she couldn't be with me one night. She had a work event. She went straight to her apartment afterward and teased me while I was at my place.

How did she tease me? She called me and made me listen to her masturbate on the phone, unable to get hard, let alone jerk a load out.

The next night, she came over with a small butt plug, which she made me shove in my ass while she toyed with me. I wanted to blow my load as I watched her strip for me. She masturbated in the shower, and the butt plug didn't give me the relief I wanted, but it helped.

For the last seven days, I've gone through countless emotions—amazement, arousal, frustration. Vanessa had no intention of giving in to my begging for a nut. I became submissive by day four. Anything she asked for, I did.

Yesterday and today, I realized this cage has helped us be more intimate without being physical. And I've enjoyed it.

However, at the end of the day, I still want her flesh. Today, I can't wait to be released.

"I want you to undress yourself," she told me as she looked into my eyes.

I wasn't dressed in much anyway. I removed myself from the sofa. I was wearing a turquoise Adidas shirt and white basketball shorts.

I did my best to be a male stripper for Vanessa. I used my mouth to be a beatbox. I danced to my own beat as I removed my shirt. She howled and cheered me on as she saw my chiseled body. I slowly took off my basketball shorts. I didn't need to hurt myself with the cock cage.

She squealed with happiness when she saw the

metallic cage. I was glad she was happy to see it because if this were any other day, my cock would have sprung from the shorts.

I stood in front of her, showing off my physique, and asked, "What's next, Vanessa?"

"I want you to undress me. Only leave my bra on."

I cleared my throat in nervousness. Vanessa looked so good in an orange slippery spaghetti strapped dress. It went well with her creme-colored skin.

She got off the sofa and flipped her curls behind her. They no longer gathered around her shoulder blades.

I tried to kiss her.

"I didn't say kiss me, Ian," she scolded me.

I rolled my eyes and rubbed my hands together to warm them up. I wanted to kiss her like I always did, but she'd ruined that. I let my hands caress her from her shoulders down to her breasts.

"Don't overwork yourself, Ian," she said. "Just undress me."

I carefully pulled the straps down her shoulders and underneath her breasts. I wanted to motorboat her and suck on her breasts, but she'd said not to remove the bra. Her bra was a soft red material. I removed the slippery dress from her stomach and down her legs. It flooded around her heels.

Her panties matched her bra. She looked like a model.

I removed the panties. Being so close to her vagina was making me weak. I reached out to her pussy. I wanted to plunge a finger or two in there. Maybe even my tongue.

"Calm down, horndog," she told me.

She'd caught me lusting.

"Just for that, I should punish you more, but I won't."

She took a seat on the sofa and instructed me to take off her heels. I did what I was told.

"Good boy," she said. I was glad she was pleased with me. I wanted to be good to be rewarded.

She told me to sit on the sofa next to her.

We started our foreplay. She was kissing me everywhere – my neck, cheeks, and stomach, but she avoided my cock.

I can't lie. I had goosebumps. If I hadn't been caged, I'd have been harder than a plank of wood.

I was moaning like a bitch, but she relished this. She told me to eat her pussy. And I did.

I ate her feverishly.

Normally, I would take my time. But this time, I was like a puppy thirsty from playing and just lapping her up quickly. I normally would put my tongue in different patterns on her pussy. Or I would take my time to focus on her clit, folds, or using my fingers on her.

I knew I was being lazy today, but I knew she understood. I couldn't believe it, but she actually orgasmed.

It was a nice thing to see, her face twisting and legs shaking because of me.

"Take off my bra," she said.

I did as I was told. I palmed her breasts before unhooking it.

Then I saw something small and silver fall out.

"What the hell?" I asked while looking between the sofa cushions. "Are you keeping coins in your bra?"

"It's something like that," she said. I could hear the smile on her lips.

"All I see is a key," I said, grabbing it.

Sarcastically, she said, "Hmmm. I forgot I left it in my bra today."

I smiled at the key and handed it to her, "Please, my keyholder. Release me."

Without hesitation, she grabbed it and used it to free me.

I felt instant pressure leave me. She told me to sit on the sofa. She grabbed a pillow, placed it on the floor, and got on her knees.

She looked like she was praying for what she was about to do for me. She firmly grabbed my cock, and I had to hold onto the arm of the chair. I felt like I was going to come from her touching me.

She saw the precum on my tip and licked it.

"Fuck!" I said as her tongue worked on the tip.

I gripped the arm harder when her mouth enveloped more than just my tip. Her mouth worked on my erection, and I told her she'd better not stop.

My hands gripped her curls as I made sure she deepthroated me. She was keeping eye contact with me, and I was about to burst.

The "gawk gawk" sound coming from Vanessa's mouth and her holding my balls while she worked on my cock was heavenly.

"Move your hands," I told her.

I held my hands on her head and shoved myself farther into her mouth. I blew my load into her mouth.

I was shocked Vanessa could swallow it all. She only missed two drops of me, and I was beyond impressed.

I expeditiously pulled her off the pillow and into my lap.

"You better ride me like this is your last rodeo," I told her.

I slid my tip between her folds to see how wet she was. She wasn't wet enough for my liking. I told her to sit on my face. I ate her like she was my favorite bowl of soup. I stroked myself, and it felt good to finally do so after a week.

Vanessa rode my face, and I think she was about to come before she stopped herself and slid down my cock.

My eyes closed as I relished being inside a pussy. My strokes are normally soft and slow, but after being caged, they were rapid and hard. Her gasps proved she wasn't expecting me to create good friction for us. I gripped her ass as we worked in unison to get to our release.

Vanessa was so damn wet it sounded like I was stirring macaroni and cheese.

She told me to not stop fucking her. She said she wanted me to explode in her. Before I could release, I saw her eyes close as her mouth did a perfect o-shape. I felt her walls clench around me as she rode herself to her completion.

The combination of her love face, gushy pussy, and her clenching allowed me to come in her hard. I growled through clenched teeth at the feeling.

We both kept still as I pulsed inside of her. She told me I was a good boy for exploding in her.

I didn't want to admit it, but I was tired. I wasn't sure if I had another load in me.

"Ian," she said as she pulled off me, "I want more of you."

"Vanessa. I can't do it," I said as I smacked her ass.

"Yes, you can," she said. "I think you need new scenery."

"New scenery?"

Vanessa said since I was tired, we could have sex in the shower. It was an easier cleanup; I could shower, then head to bed.

She walked us to the bathroom and turned on the shower. As the water got warm, we kissed and caressed each other softly.

Normally in the shower, I take the lead. But tonight, we were both on a mission. We were leaving hickeys on each other when I checked the water.

It was the perfect temperature for what we were about to do. I walked us into the shower. Our kissing sounds and moans bounced off the glass. The goosebumps I'd had earlier were nowhere to be found as she wrapped her arms around me.

My goodness! She felt softer than a baby's blanket. Her skin pressed against mine sent electric signals through my body. She was kissing me like she loved me. As a dom, she usually didn't do that.

The shower was steamy, but I think we were making our own good steam.

I kept my face in the crook of her neck to whisper sweet nothings in her ear.

She bent over with the perfect arch. I don't know how she caught a grip on the shower wall, but she did. I grabbed my cock and watched in awe as she used a free hand to spread her cheeks wide. I slipped my cock in her pussy.

She matched my medium strokes well. The steamy shower was making her lose her curls, but she didn't seem to mind. Her ass cheeks clapped loudly as she matched me. My goodness, I felt like I was going to come again.

I told her I was about to.

Her breasts bounced as I continued to give her backshots in the shower.

"You haven't lasted long at all tonight," she said. "I like that."

She had a point. It always took me longer to come than her. I guess being pent-up made me faster.

When she told me she was slipping, I listened. I made sure we were face-to-face. I carefully lifted her up and placed her on the shower wall.

I enjoyed seeing her face as I slipped myself in her pussy and gave soft strokes in her warmth. She allowed me to create the rhythm I wanted. Her breathing and squeals told me I was doing what I was supposed to do.

She called my name repeatedly as I continued to slowly stroke her. Then I felt myself get close to completion. I stroked harder and watched her breasts bounce. I came inside of the beauty.

Our foreheads connected as I caught my breath.

"Fuck!" I said. "I missed being inside of you."

"I missed that feeling too," she told me before we kissed.

After I pulled out of her, we washed each other before drying off. Then we got into our bedtime clothes for a good night's sleep.

The next morning, I woke up to soft kisses on my shoulders.

"Good morning, sleepyhead," Vanessa told me as I rolled onto my back. I felt refreshed and embraced the kisses as they traveled down my abdomen.

"What are you doing?" I asked her as I watched my dom make her way down to my penis.

My cock was as hard as steel, but I let out a breathy "Yes" as I felt her lips kiss it.

"I'm not letting a stiffy go to waste," she said before stroking my cock and sucking my balls.

What felt like an hour of her properly using her mouth and hands to work me was probably only five minutes. I tried to pull myself out of her mouth, but she refused to stop. She kept going until my nut spewed out and ran down my cock.

She decided to sit on my cock. I couldn't stop coming. She was fucking me into oblivion. My eyes were shut tightly, and I was whimpering again. She slowed down, and I was relieved.

Her movements stopped, and she placed her face on my chest.

"Are you okay?" she asked me.

"I'm fine," I told her. "You were like an Overzealous Zoey."

Her laugh came out as a snort, and she said, "I'm sorry. Your cock was hard as hell when I woke up. I had to get a piece of you."

She clenched herself against my cock, and it sent small shocks throughout my body.

She got off and went to the bedside table, where she kept a spare vibrator.

I smiled because I knew she was going to come hard using that while I was inside of her.

Vanessa got on her back, and I crawled on top of her. She put the vibrator on a low speed and wiggled it up and down her clit, then her pussy slit.

She told me she was ready for me, and I put all of my cock inside of her. She let out a large gasp and put the vibrator's head on her clit. She smiled widely as she saw me working on getting her to her climax.

I didn't want to move too fast and knock the vibrator out of her hand.

She told me she felt stuffed because of my cock and wanted to come on my cock. I told her not to hold back. My hands massaged her thighs because I didn't want her to cramp up. One of her legs was against her chest, the other wrapped around my waist.

Vanessa cursed and vigorously rubbed the vibrator on her clit as I continued to pleasure her. She squirted on me, and I was pleased at the feeling. She pushed my cock out, and I re-entered her.

Her eyes rolled to the back of her head as I felt myself about to come, but I knew to hold out for her.

She told me I'd better not come or she'd punish me later. Her thrusts matched mine as she continued to work her vibrator. I was starting to whimper again, and I think it did something for us.

"I'm coming," she told me.

"You better fucking come!" I told her, and almost on command, she convulsed against me. She took her vibrator off, but I continued to move inside her. It made her nut last longer, and I saw a smile creep onto her face.

When she came back to reality, she told me, "I

never knew having you caged would make our experiences better."

I smiled at her and told her I agreed. But I still won't be late for our next date. I want it to be a while before I'm caged again.

Still A Virgin
by Lisa Locke

"FUCK!" I EXCLAIM AS DYLAN'S COCK ENTERS my ass. "I thought you were going to be gentle."

Dylan doesn't move. I am thankful because I need to get used to the feeling.

"Lisa. I'll stop," he offers.

"Let's use more lube."

Dylan grabs some more for me and re-enters. He slowly strokes in me, and it starts to feel okay. Then it starts to feel great.

All I can think to myself is, *How the hell did I get here?*

Being a virgin isn't for the weak. Especially when you're in college.

I'm a senior at a Bible college near Boston.

However, I have dual enrollment and also attend Boston College.

I take an astronomy class at Boston College because my college doesn't offer astronomy.

Let's just say men and women hit on me all the time at Boston College. I'm five foot five, and I work out. My arms and legs are nicely toned, and my breasts are way too big for my frame.

Think of Kirstie Alley's frame on *Cheers*, but my breasts are a C-cup. I know that's small to some people, but my back says otherwise.

This doesn't mean I don't get hit on at the Bible college. Just because we attend a religious school and go to chapel doesn't mean people don't have sex.

I'm not going to lie to you, I've gotten hot and heavy before. My junior year, I actually had a boyfriend. He was sweet. A virgin like me. Our makeout sessions were intense, but we always stopped ourselves. We never did oral or anal, either.

My girlfriends have described oral to me, and it sounds sensational, but I'm waiting until marriage.

Let's take this back to August when class started.

My astronomy class was small. There were only eight of us, and I loved it. Astronomy isn't for my major; I've just always enjoyed learning about the stars and planets.

My classmates were there for different reasons, but they seemed like cool people.

I was instantly attracted to one guy in the class, Dylan. He was sweet, athletic like me, and had the face of a model. His hair was curly and went down to his shoulders.

I wanted to run my fingers through the curls.

Then in September, something straight out of a Disney Channel movie happened to Dylan and me.

My lab partner for astronomy was a nerdy guy named Justin. The good thing about Justin was he was not overly nerdy, and he made astronomy more fun. I was bummed out when he texted me thirty minutes before one lab to let me know he was sick and couldn't make it.

I had to join another lab group. However, Dylan's lab partner was sick, too, and we paired up.

If you looked in the dictionary at the word "attractive," Dylan's name and face would be by it. His bronze skin is radiant. His eyelashes are long and thick. His lips look juicer than a Starburst. He always wears a long-sleeved shirt or a hoodie and jeans to class. The shirts barely conceal his muscular build.

I maintained my cool during the lab. I managed to focus on the work. He did, too, but we both have a sense of humor, so jokes were made.

I told him I was a 22-year-old senior. He let me know he was a 21-year-old junior.

After lab, we exchanged numbers. We parted ways, and I went to the bus stop. He hopped into his Jeep.

Over the next few weeks, we would text and call each other. It wasn't an everyday thing, but a few times a week. My face would always light up at hearing his voice or reading his text messages.

One day after lab, he waited with me at the bus stop until the bus arrived.

"I hope you know I enjoy talking with you," he said.

"I enjoy talking with you, too," I told him.

"I would like to take you on a date."

I'm sure my face was pinker than Pepto Bismol.

"I know I look skinny, but I like to eat more than just salads. I need a roast beef sandwich."

He laughed and said, "I love to eat too. You don't have to worry about that."

The next week, classes kicked my ass. I also had a part-time job. I was so stressed that week, that I masturbated three times. I normally flick my bean only once a week. College is pressure, and I needed relief.

Let's just say that each time I did, I used Dylan as the leading man in my fantasy. I always imagined that he would know how to use his lips to satisfy a woman.

The school week went by so fast. The weekend came, and I wasn't surprised when lab class came back around.

Justin and I worked hard on our lab assignment, but Dylan couldn't keep his eyes off me. I walked over to him and told him to focus.

"Your beauty radiates through the room," he said. "I can't help it."

I'll tell you one thing. I know he genuinely liked me, but he knows how to talk well.

After lab, he offered me a ride so I didn't have to wait for the bus. You would think that after all these years in college, I'd be comfortable getting into a car with a boy. Sadly, I'm not. It takes a while to get my trust.

I know people think Christians are oblivious to the world around them, but my folks taught me how to be more than a church mouse.

What Dylan did next shocked me.

He actually waited at the bus stop with me. Then he took the bus with me.

He asked me if I was ready for tomorrow's date. I

told him I was ready to learn more about him on the date.

Instead of pressuring me and following me to my dorm, he saw me get dropped off at the well-lit student union where other students were.

He stayed on the bus and asked me to call him when I was safe. I did just that when I arrived at my room.

I was really starting to like him, and I knew he liked me. But our date solidified this for me.

I've been on dates before, but it was refreshing being with Dylan.

I didn't have to touch a door; he pulled out my chair and pushed it in, I wasn't worried about the check, he didn't get on me about eating a lot of food, and our conversations were meaningful. He told me his short-term and long-term goals. He told me what he likes to see in healthy relationships. I think I really hit the jackpot. I didn't want to jinx myself, though.

Afterward, we went back to the student union at my college. He pulled Monopoly out of the trunk of his car.

"Finances are my thing," I told him. "I'll be wealthy by the end of the game."

"I'll believe it when I see it," he told me.

The game went well. I noticed what type of financial decisions he made. He may not be a long-term man in my life, but I needed to know where his head was at when it comes to money.

I won, by the way.

By October, we started dating. It wasn't easy balancing school, work, and dating. We managed it, though.

He came into my room a lot and studied with me. I studied at the apartment he shared with a classmate. Dylan knows how to cook, and his food is to die for.

Let's not forget the nights when we lay together and watched a movie. There were several nights when my body didn't know how to act around him.

My nipples would be erect. I'd go home with wet panties from my arousal. His cock had a mind of its own too. I would feel it when we napped together. We danced a lot on our nights alone. I would feel his erection then too.

On nights when our kissing got out of hand, our hands couldn't get enough of each other, and he would stop us.

"It's too soon," he told me. I was shocked to hear him say that.

I was the virgin. I mean, he didn't know I was a virgin. But he would ask me to give him time. He said he always moved too fast when it came to sex.

Which was fine by me. But my Lord, our chemistry was there! I know we wanted to jump each other's bones, but we refrained.

Then came Halloween.

When everybody was dressed like Jessica Rabbit, sexy nurses, and ghouls just to hook up with strangers, we went to my place, and I confessed to him.

"I pled to stay a virgin until I am married," I told him.

"No way you're a virgin," he told me.

This was typically everyone's reaction when I told them.

I expected him to call me a prude or too pretty to be a virgin.

"I thought you were having sex already. I know this sounds sexist, but with your shape, you look like you fuck good."

"Dylan!" I exclaimed, shocked at his response. "You can't tell if someone is good at sex based on their physique."

"I suppose so. But you also have a great confidence about you."

"So because I have confidence, I'm supposed to be good at sex?" I asked him.

"Sorry. I need to be more open-minded."

I couldn't fault the guy. Many people had their opinions about virgins.

"I can't lie to you," he said. "I don't want to have sex right now, but I'm not sure if I can wait until marriage. I know that's a lot of pressure on you, but I have to be honest."

"I don't know what to say," I told him.

"I don't know what to say either," he said. "I don't want to break up with you. But I don't want to have sex with anyone else, either. Especially when our connection is so strong."

"Let's just see where this goes," I said. "We just have to keep living the way we have. Focus on school, focus on work, and focus on each other. We can focus on each other without sex. Like what we've been doing."

He agreed.

Thanksgiving break came, and we were thankful for a break from university life. Even though exams were ten days later, Dylan and I were glad to take a breather. He actually met my family the day after Thanksgiving. We were going to see a blockbuster film, and Dylan was interested in it.

He met us for lunch, and he blended in well with my siblings and parents. He was actually himself and wasn't trying to be fake. My parents aren't super strict Christians, so it worked.

After lunch, we went to the movies. Being there with him and my family felt right. After the movie was over, my family talked about interesting themes and symbols in the movie. Let's just say, it was like Dylan was a longtime family friend.

December arrived in a blink. We finished exams, and it was time to leave campus. Because of my work-study job, I was eligible to stay on campus for another week after exams.

Dylan picked me up after work because he was heading home for break in a few days, but we wanted alone time in the car.

"We're fogging up the windows," he said, breaking up our makeout session.

"I'm sorry," I said, seeing his cock print in his gray sweatpants.

"Let's calm down," he said, adjusting us.

It took us a minute to calm down, but we did.

"I'm beyond interested in you," Dylan said. "But I badly want to fuck you."

I started blushing and cleared my throat. "I want to fuck you, too, but I know we can hold out."

"But I cannot hold out two to three years from now when we get married," he said.

You know I geeked out on the inside when he said that.

"But we have other things to tend to first," Dylan added. "I'm looking forward to you meeting my parents."

"Oh yes!" I said. "I know I'll have them wrapped around my finger."

He chuckled. "I bet you will. They're easy folks to be around."

The days went by, and it was the day after Christmas.

My lust to have him as my first was strong. I was trying to subdue my thoughts daily, but the small things made me feel like I should give in. I'm sure he felt the same way, but he held it in for me.

I have been watching porn for years, and I have an idea of what sex should feel like, but I was ready for the real thing. I was ready for his cock to be inside of me.

For days, I prayed that meeting his parents would calm down my lust.

I met his parents, and it was a great time. Because they are great cooks, I now knew where he got it from. Dylan doesn't have siblings; it's just him.

His parents offered to let me stay the night. But I

declined. I knew Dylan, and I might give in to lust. I didn't want to take the walk of shame at his parents' house.

While in the room with him, I said, "Technically, I'm still a virgin if you fuck me in the ass…"

"I have never done that before," Dylan said.

"But I want you inside of me."

"But in the ass, baby? That's wild." He laughed. "I'll see what we can do."

I made a gleeful smile and hugged him.

We parted ways that night. But I needed to research anal.

* * *

Which brings us to today. It's New Year's Eve, and we are at his apartment lounging around. It feels good to be with him for a whole day and not just half a day because of work or school.

Dylan has also helped me be adventurous today. We were getting ourselves comfortable with the idea of anal. I did research all week by reading several health sites for women.

Don't get me wrong. I'm nervous as hell. Dylan's cock is girthy, and I know it's eight inches long. He allowed me to be curious and measure him.

We just got out of the shower, where he comfortably fingered my ass. It was good practice. Besides, we were naked, and I loved it. I know people would think that since I'm a virgin and Christian, I would prefer being clothed, but I love nakedness.

Now seeing him naked and his cock responding to me, I am pleased.

While being naked in his apartment, I did get chilly. Let's just say Dylan knew how to warm me up. He wrapped his arms around my torso as he kissed me from my ear down to my collarbone. My body quivered at his actions, even though I was warming up.

He did the same thing to the other side of my body, and I could feel positive energy run to my nipples to get erect.

My instant response was to twist my nipples, and I'm glad I did.

He removed my hands and cupped my breasts in his hands so he could suck each nipple separately. I let out a gasp from the sensation, and I was starting to get wet.

This was a different experience from when I watch porn because usually, I have to give foreplay to myself to keep myself wet.

I walked us over to the bed, and his lips continued their journey down my body. His hands still multitasked and touched spots that I didn't realize would send me into a frenzy.

He told me he was going to eat me out today.

I've had many boyfriends over the years who wanted to do that to me, but I never did because they weren't special enough for that type of intimacy. Besides, it's not sex—right?

Dylan is the first. It's the reason why I'm comfortable doing anal with him.

When his lips trail to my thighs to kiss on me, once again, my nipples react instantly. I play with my breasts as he kisses my pussy lips. His lips vibrate on the sensitive piece of flesh, and my body jolts.

My eyes open wide as I feel his thick tongue spread my pussy lips open. My goodness, it is a sensational feeling to be spread wide with his tongue cooling down my pussy. I feel tingles all over my body as I watch him suck and slurp me like I'm a meal.

When he puts one finger in my pussy and another in my ass, I almost come. But his actions aren't rough. He continues to take his time with me. He knows I am okay because of the moans. I softly rub on my clit as he does all of this, and I come.

I'm not ashamed as he sees me come undone.

He slowly withdraws his fingers. I'm glad he does

because I feel empty and sad. He grabs some lubricant for himself and says, "I want you to put it on me."

He squirts lubricant in my hand, and I warm it up and distribute it from his tip down to his shaft.

Dylan tells me he loves seeing his cock in my hand. It hardens fast, and he says, "We can back out."

"No, the hell we're not," I say, getting comfortable on the bed.

I get on all fours, and he smacks my ass before putting his tip in.

"Fuck!" I exclaim as it goes in. "I thought you were going to be gentle."

Dylan stops moving. I am thankful because I need to get used to the feeling.

"Lisa. I'll stop," he offers.

"Let's use more lube."

Dylan grabs some more for me and re-enters. He slowly strokes me, and it starts to feel okay. Then it starts to feel great.

"Don't clench," he tells me as he gives me more of his cock.

I feel stretched as hell. His strokes are still gentle, and before I know it, I've helped us gain a rhythm. It feels so good having him back there. He tells me I am doing a good job, and he can't believe how good it feels.

We are moaning in harmony as he speeds up his strokes. I feel so damn comfortable I don't want it to end.

He slowly pulls out of me and lays me on my side. Then he enters my ass again.

"Fuck!" he said as we lay sideways. "Arch yourself a little more," he says as his hand helps me create an arch in my back.

We both curse in unison at how good a simple move feels. I love hearing our skin clap together as his cock works me.

"I'm gonna come," he tells me.

"Please," I beg him.

Dylan whimpers like a puppy as he comes inside of me, and I can feel the hot fluid fill up my ass. I smile, knowing I got him to that moment.

He slowly pulls out of me and starts kissing me.

"Fuck! It felt good releasing in you."

He holds me tight as we lie on his covers, and he kisses me.

He checks in on me. I tell him I am a little sore, but I'm happy to know what anal feels like. I now know vaginal sex will be amazing with him.

"And I'm still a virgin."

The Physical
by Jade St. James

"CARMEN, YOU HAVE TO PERK UP," PEDRO SAID while he and his girlfriend were on their morning jog.

"I know I have to, babe," she said. "But I only have a few more days with you. Today's Saturday, and by Wednesday morning, you will be shipped off to California."

"But we knew this was going to happen," he said as they jogged back to her apartment.

"I know," she said. "Time flew by, is all."

The dark-skinned woman grabbed her keys from her pocket and let them into the apartment.

Pedro started speaking to her in Spanish to calm her down.

Once the door closed, Pedro looked down to talk

to her. His dark-toned hands reached out to hers, but she didn't want to listen to him.

He spoke in English. "I know these next few days will go by fast, but we will cherish them. We'll make the long-distance work. My Army salary is now higher, so if I have to pay to visit you or for you to come to me, it'll be worth it."

Carmen tried to smile, but tears were about to drop from her eyes. She placed her head on his chest for comfort, and he held her.

"Let it out," he told her as he hugged her.

Carmen's boyfriend Pedro was shipping off with the Army in a few days. Since they weren't married, Carmen couldn't go with him to California. Besides, she was deep in her third year of medical school on the East Coast.

The two had only been together for a year, but it had been one of the healthiest relationships in Carmen's short life. They were both 24, but Pedro had been in the Army since he was 18.

This was his first time being with a woman like Carmen, and he wasn't ready to leave her. This situation could go so many ways—long-distance issues, cheating, or money problems.

But Pedro had made up his mind: positivity only. He didn't need them to think negatively.

"We need to shower and start our day," she said, pulling herself away from him. "Separately."

Pedro was a little offended, but he knew she needed alone time. He started breakfast while she showered.

Carmen cried in the shower. They'd literally found out a week ago that he had to leave. He'd been packing ever since. She felt like she shouldn't cry over their 12 months together; they were still a new couple. But something about him made her feel like he was marriage material.

All she could think about was being lonely in the apartment. Yes. Her roommate was still there, but she had seen Pedro twice a week for the last year. Or sometimes they would spend a whole week together at his place. Now she was probably only going to see him once a quarter.

That meant probably only having sex once a quarter.

She knew sex probably should have been the last thing on her mind, but it wasn't. Carmen didn't know how, but the five men she'd had sex with had all been great lovers. Pedro was number five, and she craved his loving often.

She cleared her thoughts once she could smell the food he was cooking. Her stomach grumbled, and she took that as her cue to finish washing and get dressed.

They ate the simple but tasty breakfast–canned corn beef, toast, and roasted potatoes.

Afterward, he went to shower, and they prepared for their day.

The couple was getting professional photos done. His parents and little brother lived two states away and were going to fly in today and leave Monday evening.

Then for dinner, Carmen and Pedro's mother were going to collaborate on a home-cooked meal for him.

When Pedro came out of the shower and dressed, he looked so good to Carmen. He was wearing an emerald button-down with black dress pants. Pedro loved seeing her in her emerald cocktail dress. It barely touched her knees, and he wanted to bend her over in the dress, but he knew they had somewhere important to be.

They headed to the photography studio.

The rest of the day was a whirlwind by the time they met his family at the airport.

Pedro thought dinner was wonderful, and he loved that his mother and Carmen had done it for him. He also loved seeing his mom practice Spanish with Carmen.

After dinner, everyone worked together to clean up. Pedro gave his family the key to his apartment.

"You all head back to my place," he told them. "I have to pack another box real quick. I'll be over."

"That's weird as hell," his 18-year-old brother said. "We'll wait for you, bro."

"Naw. I have this box to pack, and Carmen's been getting on me about it. I'll be home in thirty."

Carmen had no clue what he was talking about but followed along.

His family gave in and headed toward his apartment.

"Pedro. What box do we have to pack?"

"We don't. I just wanted to check in on you. This morning you were distraught. You perked up during the day, and I was glad. But I still wanted to check in."

Carmen smiled at how healthy their relationship was.

"I'm in a way better place than this morning. The photos made me feel better. Seeing your folks made me feel better. I know pouting isn't the answer to this. You are willing to put in the work, and I am too."

Pedro lifted Carmen up and twirled her around. She squealed, and he told her he was glad she was getting comfortable with the idea.

Saturday night was practically over, and Wednesday morning, he had to leave.

"I also wanted to know if I could pack your box with my dick," he said, kissing her face.

"Yes," she said, kissing him back. "But we only fifteen minutes, and you're not a quick pumper."

"Don't worry about me," he said, leaving pecks on her lips.

She was so glad her roommate didn't get off until midnight.

Pedro helped Carmen undress, then he put her on the kitchen table, ate her pussy, and packed her box.

He wasn't used to quickies. She told him everything had to be fast. He increased his speed to get her to climax. He loved watching her as she came on his dick. He actually saw the relief on her face, and he smiled.

"Fantasy unlocked," he said as he pulled himself out of her.

"A quickie on the kitchen table is a fantasy of yours?"

"Yes," he said. "And you fulfilled it."

She started blushing and said, "I'm glad I did that for you. Any others?"

He helped her off the table, and she got dressed as he admitted another fantasy.

"I've always wanted to have a beautiful female

doctor do my annual military physical. I expect her to strip me down and inspect my body."

"No way!" she said, being playful. "Noted."

The two walked to her room and "packed" a small box with frivolous things to take to his apartment.

They kissed, and she watched him leave.

The next day was Sunday. Instead of going to church, Carmen took Pedro's family to her university. They loved seeing the historic area where she was continuing her education. Afterward, they went to play laser tag and finally had a big dinner at a restaurant.

Carmen said goodnight to everyone when they dropped her off at the apartment. Once inside, she showered and did some online shopping. She needed to get Pedro a going-away gift. They'd had cute selfie photos printed, but she wanted to finally put them together.

She went on Amazon and ordered a small photo album, a doctor's costume, and lingerie underneath. Pedro wasn't going to be ready for what she had planned for him.

Monday morning, Carmen didn't want to go to class, but she mustered up the energy. It was 7:30 a.m., and she did her morning routine.

As she finished brushing her teeth, she received a call from Pedro.

"Baby. I need to be inside of you," he said once she answered.

"Pedro. We don't have time. I have to leave by 8:45 for my 9:30 class."

That's when he told her he was in her parking lot with an erection.

Carmen paused as she thought about what to do next. She gave in. Because after next week, she knew she'd crave him and wouldn't have the opportunity to have him in her.

She unlocked the door for him, and he swooped her up. He practically ran to the room before instructing her in Spanish to give him head. He needed her mouth on his seven inches or else he wouldn't feel complete.

After getting his dick slippery, she spread her legs wide and told him, "Come and get it."

Tuesday morning, she was ready for class. Sadly, she knew this was her last day with her boyfriend. He was leaving tomorrow morning. Instead of leaving at 6 a.m. like a responsible person, he was leaving around 9 a.m. She told him to do this because he was going to need to sleep in.

She would give him his gift tonight, but also fulfill his fantasy.

It was 7:30 a.m., and she texted him, "Come to Room 104 at the hospital at 9 p.m. A physical exam is required for all recruits."

She worked at a small community hospital in the area. There were always two empty rooms, and the cameras didn't always catch movement there.

Carmen knew what she had planned was illegal, and she might lose everything she worked for, but she wanted a final night of passion with him.

She sometimes closed with a coworker that never knew what is going on. She was always clueless.

So Carmen and Pedro had enough time to do what they needed. Carmen wanted to make him come at least three times.

Pedro arrived at the hospital saying he had a physical scheduled with Carmen.

Staff told him it was unusual for a physical that late but that he would be in good hands with Carmen.

When he arrived, she treated him like a stranger. Her coworkers had never met him before, and this worked in their favor. When he got to the room, he instantly loved seeing her in a doctor's uniform.

Instinctively, he wrapped his arms around her torso.

"You look so damn fuckable," he said as he felt his dick stiffen.

She showed him what she had on underneath.

"Lingerie? Baby, what are you doing? We'll get caught."

"It's role play. We won't get caught. My coworker is a Ditzy Dianne. We just can't be loud. All right. This physical includes a prostate exam, erection exam, and stamina exam."

She stripped him of his clothes, and he loved seeing her in charge.

She softly pushed him into a wall in the room. He looked down at her as she started kissing him from his v-cuts up to his lips, then traveling back down to his dick before putting it in her mouth.

"Shit!" he said through gritted teeth. He told the "doctor" to suck his dick like it was a lollipop. She did as she was told. When his dick was as slippery as a wet floor, Carmen pulled out a butt plug out of her bookbag and said, "Prostate exam first."

Pedro had a love-hate relationship with butt plugs. He only liked them on days when he wanted to come fast. But other times, he could live without it because he preferred to pleasure Carmen and make her come multiple times.

He practically salivated as he watched her perform oral on the butt plug. He stroked his dick at the sight before she inserted the plug in him.

"You're passing the erection exam," she said before giving him head. His eyes closed in bliss as she twisted her hands around his dick with his sensitive mushroom-shaped tip in her mouth. The slow vibrations of the plug worked with her to help him get to his climax.

Her slurping was loud, but no one came to check on them. Pedro kept his moans low. It was only a matter of minutes before she tasted his pre-cum. Yes, her arms and mouth were tired, but she maintained the same motions as he told her, "I'm gonna come in your mouth."

His hands roamed his upper torso, and he planted his feet as he felt himself come in her mouth.

She pulled him out and stroked him longer, and let the rest of the cum coat her breasts.

After he came, she pulled the plug out of him and let him gain composure. She did notice his dick was starting to get soft. She pulled off her doctor's coat and fully showed the mustard lingerie on her.

His dick started to rise again. She knew he was going to pass the erection portion.

"You passed the prostate and erection exams," she said, cleaning the sticky cum off her breasts.

"Doctor," he said, getting her attention.

Their eyes locked, and he pleaded, "Please tell me it's time for the stamina exam. I know I will outperform."

"You'd better fucking perform, recruit," she said.

In the bedlike reclining chair, Pedro bent her over and put half of his dick in her. She buried her face in the leather fabric of the chair to muffle her moans. For the next seven minutes in heaven, doggy style was the thing. The backshots were soft and sensual.

He knew if he was fast and furious, the remaining staff would hear their skin slapping.

His hands fondled her titties as he helped her pleasure herself. She came so hard from it, he had to cover her mouth as she called his name.

One of the sturdier chairs in the room was the next spot for the stamina exam. He sat in it and pulled her down on his dick.

They both cursed in Spanish as he forced her movements on his dick. She was sliding up and down him like a stripper on a pole. She clenched her pussy around him several times. He fucked her a little harder because he felt like he was going to come.

"Get on your knees, doctor," he said, slowing down his movements. She got off of him and opened her mouth wide. Her big pretty eyes were glued to seeing him stroke his dick.

She wanted to swallow all of his kids.

Pedro was careful not to be loud as he stuffed his dick in her mouth as she swallowed the hot cum.

She sucked him until he pulled out of her mouth.

He needed to come in her missionary. It was his favorite position to give her a creampie.

Space was limited, but she balanced herself at an angle on the edge of the leather medical chair and slipped him inside her pussy.

They both covered their mouths to muffle the gasps they emitted.

He used her thighs for leverage to massage her pussy as he kissed her nasty and slow. His dick did all of the talking as Pedro and Carmen kissed. This position had him hitting the right spot, and she told him not to stop until he came.

She said he was passing the stamina exam, but it wasn't over until he came. She looked down at his movements and said, "I love seeing you inside of me."

That was something he loved to hear. He worked on her pussy for a few more minutes before telling her he was coming.

"Look me in my eyes," she told him.

Her big glossy eyes always got him. It did something to him that he couldn't figure out, but he continued to swim in her tight pussy as she looked up at him and begged him to come in her.

His dick twitched as he came inside of her. He carefully pulled out of her, a bit of his cum still oozing.

They kissed feverishly.

"You fucking passed the stamina exam," she told him.

The two got dressed, cleaned up their surroundings, and sanitized every surface they'd used. They washed their hands.

She checked off stuff on his paper and walked out in her normal work clothes. A few moments later, he walked out and thanked the staff.

He could tell they had no idea what had transpired in that room, and he was thankful. He drove to his place to shower because Carmen would be off the clock in thirty. When she came by his place, she showered too.

The couple could not stop talking about the sexcapade they'd had.

Hell! Pedro desired more, but he needed rest for his two-day drive.

Once she came out of the shower in her pajamas, she passed him his gift. She'd put it in a box and wrapped it in Snoopy wrapping paper. Snoopy was his favorite cartoon character.

He started crying after he opened the box and flipped through the photos of him and her. The photos ranged from their third date to off-guards they'd taken at family events, him in his uniform, them at a concert, and them in the kitchen cooking together.

The more time they spent together, the more he realized she was marriage material. But he cleared his thoughts when he saw the final set of pictures in the album.

There were a few risqué photos of her with different hairstyles and makeup looks. She was clothed in the photos, but everything else was suggestive—eating a banana, her body oiled, her sitting on a dildo, and his favorite was her in a sudsy bathtub.

He repeatedly thanked her and said he couldn't wait to make more memories with her.

"Thank you for fulfilling my fantasy," he said.

"Anytime you need a physical, I got you, baby," she said.

Surprise at the Front Door
by Scotty Barnes

TOM MET VANESSA AT THE DOOR AND inquired, "Ready to fuck?"

She was curvy, gorgeous, and ready to fuck. They'd been flirting online for weeks, and they finally got their schedules to line up. She was good to go.

It was 10 p.m., and as the saying goes, "After 10, he's trying to get in."

He was so glad Vanessa looked like her profile picture. She resembled Brooke Elliott from *Drop Dead Diva*.

Vanessa was thankful he matched his profile—lean, muscular, and an attractive face like a young Brendan Fraser.

They started kissing before the front door even

closed. James could hear their smooching noises from the other room.

In haste, her clothes started coming off. She was barely wearing any clothes anyway—she was wearing biker shorts and a tight camisole. No underwear or bra on at all.

As Tom reached down to take off his shoes, he spotted a man sitting in the living room, watching them.

What the fuck?

Vanessa saw Tom's body language change.

"Oh, that's just my husband, James," she said calmly. "I thought he'd learn a lot by watching a real man fuck me."

Tom paused.

This was not what he'd signed up for. She should have told him!

"Why didn't you tell me you're married? I only have sex with single women," he said. He was glad the only thing off of him was his shirt. "I thought you and I were going somewhere with this relationship, Vanessa."

Tom was not going to let some guy watch him fuck. No way!

"He's a cuckold," she said. "He needs to learn how to fuck a full-figured woman."

"No," Tom said, backing away from her. He needed to think because he'd enjoyed talking with her the last few weeks, and he still wanted to fuck her.

While he paused to figure out what to do, Vanessa quickly got on her knees to unbutton and unzip his jeans.

He wasn't wearing any underwear.

She couldn't believe he was already hard and put his dick in her mouth. He protested, but it felt too good.

James approached. "My wife is a fucking goddess, and she deserves a hard fuck, from a big-dicked stud like you. You would be doing me a favor."

This was too much for Tom. The man called him a "big-dicked stud." While Tom knew he was packing a third leg, he didn't need James to tell him.

Tom zipped up his jeans, grabbed his shirt and shoes off the floor, and walked out of the house. On the steps, he grappled with the possibility of staying.

He was already rock-hard. He had also driven 45 minutes to get there. All week, she'd talked about having him inside of her.

He timidly walked back inside to see Vanessa naked on the rug, legs spread. James said, "At least taste my wife's pussy?"

How did they know I'd be back? he thought to himself.

And thus begins a weird and wild night of fucking.

Tom didn't even let his eyes veer toward James, but he stared Vanessa down like a hawk. He swiftly walked to the rug and sat down.

She was a grand sight to see. Her breasts were the size of cantaloupes, her nipples were already erect, her wide hips caught his attention, and finally, he saw the golden spot—her honey pot.

Her clit was pronounced and protruding. Her honey pot lips were as bright as a pink Starburst. While on his knees, he spread her legs wide for more access and dipped his tongue into her folds.

She let out a wispy sigh as his cool tongue worked on her.

Vanessa gripped a handful of the rug as his lips sucked her clit. James rubbed on her breasts as Tom continued to feast on her warm and wet honeypot. He slipped a finger in her, and she squirted on his hand.

That was all the motivation he needed.

"I need to be in you now," he said.

Vanessa watched in awe as he got undressed. She fingered herself to stay wet for him. Her gushiness permeated the small room and made Tom's dick harder.

"Don't you fucking come yet," Tom ordered her.

He stroked his dick as he started to eat her honeypot like it was a ripe, juicy watermelon.

"James. You need to learn how to eat the way he does," she said in between her haggard breathing.

She started screeching Tom's name, and finally came into his mouth.

While she enjoyed her orgasm, he grabbed a condom out of his jeans pocket and put it on his dick.

Just like in the videos he'd sent her, his dick had weight to it. Not only did it have length, but thickness. His dick was like a Rogerwood sausage.

Off her high, she spoke up.

"Damn, James. You'll never measure up to what he has. You wouldn't know what to do with all that dick," she demeaned him.

Tom sat on the rug and spread his legs wide as his dick stood tall like the skyscrapers in New York.

He called her over. She crawled to her lover and straddled him. He kissed the beautiful woman as she made sure to use her hands to keep him hard. He loved thick women, and he loved how heavy she felt in his arms.

Tom slightly lifted her up, and on cue, she inserted his dick in her honeypot.

Instantly, her eyes rolled to the back of her head as she felt herself stretch to accommodate him.

James loved seeing this. She usually didn't make a sexy, twisted face when he entered her.

Vanessa managed to look at James and said, "You could never fill me up like this."

Tom loosely wrapped his arms around her torso as he gazed into her eyes. The woman knew how to bounce on his dick as they kept eye contact.

Vanessa knew she was doing all the work at the moment, but she didn't mind. Mainly because by now, James would have come already, and round one was done in two minutes.

Not with Tom. Tom was focusing on the sweet spots she'd told him she had. She ground on him while he was inside of her. The two both moaned and grunted through the actions.

Tom held her in place and thrust upward in her hard and fast. She squealed in response to him taking control, and she didn't want it any other way.

"James, take notes," she managed to say.

The two worked together to make each other feel good. Tom felt like he was in a narrow river approaching a waterfall. He was paddling to keep up with her, and he knew he would reach the waterfall eventually. Tom was getting closer to the edge.

He didn't want to ruin their rhythm, but it was harder not to go over that edge. He knew this was a balancing act. Her actions and noises proved that this felt good to her too. He wondered if she could tell he was getting close.

While he maintained himself, she gripped her legs around his waist tighter, and he felt her body shudder as she came on his dick.

"Fuck me through it," she coached him as he didn't stop his movement.

He was relieved that she had made it there, but this also meant he could come too.

Tom placed his hands on her hips and created the speed he needed. The man clutched her hips harder and came.

"Fuck, Vanessa," he drawled out.

The woman didn't stop stroking him with her honeypot until she noticed he came from his pinnacle.

The couple forgot James was there until he passed them a small trash can for the condom.

"Are you staying?" Vanessa asked Tom as she carefully got off him.

"Hell yes," he said, grabbing another condom.

Vanessa took this chance to demean James again.

"James. He gets hard faster than you. Tom has the stamina for me," she said.

Tom smacked her ass because hearing her talk like that was a turn-on.

She grabbed his dick and led them to her sofa with the ottoman. She noticed James was now naked and hard. She told him he was only allowed to come once while he watched her and Tom.

James looked at the couple again.

Once again, Tom couldn't keep his hands and lips off her curves. She was a curvy road he could drive on all night.

"Doggystyle, please?" she asked as he put on the new condom.

"Hell yeah," he said, pushing her on all fours on the ottoman.

He seized her ass cheeks in his hand and spread them wide as he sucked her honeypot a bit.

One hand on her ass cheek, his dick in the other, he knocked on the entrance to her honeypot.

"Come in," she said.

Tom's whole dick slid in with ease, but it reminded Vanessa that his dick was still a heavy hitter.

She told James about how good it felt to have a real man inside her. How good it felt to experience a big dick for a change.

"Fuck me in front of my husband," she said as he

created a pattern of movements that was driving them both wild.

She was so damn wet, he slipped out, and she said, "Please give it back."

Tom used different depths and rhythms to find a balance for them.

Every thrust he gave brought waves of pleasurable sensations to his dick. His heartbeat increased with his breathing. She responded back to each thrust with a kegel. He felt a strong tension on the base of his penis.

He was going to come again.

He kept going with forceful thrusts.

"Oh shit!" she called out as he positioned her hands behind her back and kept with the rough shots.

Both of them were out of breath. It wasn't long before they were coming together.

It felt like an earth-shaking orgasm for Tom. He couldn't believe they'd united as one when they came. It was like a breath of fresh air.

They heard James come over himself when they finished their shared moment.

It kind of turned Vanessa on.

Tom held her in his arms and kissed every inch of her he could reach. Then he pulled out and disposed of the rubber.

"Let's go to the master bedroom," she told him.

Tom couldn't believe she wanted more. He grabbed the final condom and followed her like a lost puppy.

James trailed the couple to the bedroom.

Tom watched her every move as she crawled into the queen-sized bed that she normally shared with her husband.

"What a shame," Tom said. "Your wife's fucking another man in the bed you share with her. Fucking cuckold."

James knew he was right, but at the moment, he just wanted to view his wife get stretched by Tom.

This time, Vanessa put the condom on him, and he liked seeing her rip the package open with her teeth.

She lay on her back and guided his dick in her honeypot.

Just like in previous times, Tom knew how to work her body like a skilled man.

"You fucking see this, James?" she taunted her husband.

Tom started to get into it, joining in on the taunting—which James loved.

"Your wife takes my dick like a good bitch," Tom said.

This is what he'd always wanted—seeing his wife enjoy someone other than him.

Vanessa watched Tom maneuver himself into her folds and said, "Use my pussy to come all over me."

"I fucking will," he told her as he placed his face in her breasts.

She called Tom's name out repetitively.

"Choke me in front of my husband," she said.

Tom choked her and asked, "Too much?"

His grip was firm and not too restrictive, and she told him, "Just like this."

After a few strokes, he removed his hand and used her love handles for leverage.

"I'm about to come," he told her.

Once again, she said, "Use my pussy to come all over me."

Tom loved how much of a motivator she was. He pulled out of her honeypot and quickly removed the rubber to come over her melons.

Vanessa loved it and cheered this on.

James loved watching her reactions to this.

Tom kissed Vanessa on the lips and said, "I need a shower."

She gave a head nod in the direction of the bathroom.

James was hard as hell and fucked his wife while Tom was in the shower.

Tom couldn't believe the wild night he was having.

As a single man, this was one of the weirdest nights of his life. On top of that, he couldn't believe he was enjoying it.

But Vanessa made it worth it.

In the shower, all he could think about was her.

While he dried off, the couple came into the shower. He removed himself from the equation and walked back to the living room, where his clothes were.

He fell asleep on the sofa in the clothes he came with.

* * *

The next morning, when Tom awoke, Vanessa was asleep next to him. He must have been dog-tired because he didn't know she'd even joined him.

James came into the living room and said he wanted to see them together one final time before he went to work.

"What do you want to see?" Vanessa asked her husband.

"Doggy again."

Vanessa sprang into action with Tom. Their kissing session was quick and fierce. She threw a blanket on the floor and arched her back for Tom to enter her.

Tom couldn't believe he was having raw sex with her. Just like the many times in the last 12 hours, she responded well to his strokes.

It wasn't long before the two came together in unison.

James loved seeing this. He wanted to stay, but he had to go to work.

James said to Tom, "Thank you for dicking her down good. I hope she can see you again."

Tom looked into Vanessa's eyes and said, "I would love to see you again." If she was going to fuck him like this regularly, he definitely wanted to see her again.

He went to the bathroom for another shower. Meanwhile, Vanessa and James had a private conversation near the door.

Vanessa kissed James goodbye and told him to have a great day at work.

"I fucking love you, cuckold," she said.

Personal Trainer
by Peter Barash

"I WOULD LICK THE SWEAT OFF HIS ASS," Tanya said, looking at Ivan.

"Girl! I'd do squats on his dick until he told me to stop," said Jackie.

"Oh, my God!" Carly said. "I'll be his personal rowing machine."

All three gossiping women cackled and watched Ivan as he worked out by himself, oblivious to what the women were saying.

Ivan was a personal trainer at the gym. He was 22, in amazing shape, and the topic of discussion among all the women at the gym.

And he loved it.

It was good for his ego—which was pretty substantial, to begin with.

The women wanted his personal training so they could lose weight. His face and physique were the icing on the cake.

They wanted to be stretched by him—including him stretching their vaginas.

When a person signed up for personal training at the gym, they got an uninterrupted hour with Ivan including 15 minutes of stretching.

He had green eyes, a small beard, and hair like Noah Syndergaard. He had to be at least 6 feet tall.

Tanya, Jackie, and Carly were three divorced women in their 40s, and they all wanted to fuck him. Especially Carly, even more than Tanya and Jackie.

She was a mom of two and had been divorced for two years. The other two women had each been divorced for less than a year.

Carly didn't want to have sex that first year; plus, she was balancing being a single mom. Now her vagina meowed at the sight of any man that was attractive like Ivan. She was so glad when she found out he was over 21. She herself was 40 and didn't want to rob the cradle.

"I'll get him in my bed before you bitches," Jackie said competitively.

"Oh, please," Tanya said. "He looks like he likes

Black women. So I have a better chance with him than you or Carly.

"I have a little Asian flavor to give him," Carly said. "I signed up for his sessions last week so I'll get him first."

The other two women dropped their jaws as Carly walked to her car.

* * *

The next day, the women went swimming for exercise, and Jackie said, "Let's make a bet that whoever jumps his bones first gets a relaxation day on the two losers. The two losers have to keep the winner's kids for a whole day."

"I won't refuse that," Carly said.

"I wouldn't either," Tanya said. "I know my kids get tired of seeing me."

The women shook hands and said, "Deal."

All three laughed at themselves for behaving like horny teenage girls and went back to swimming.

* * *

Carly woke up for her Monday morning workout with Ivan. She didn't want to get out of bed, but she didn't have her kids this week. Hell! She was only going to see them a few times this summer because they were at sports camps and spending time with their dads.

The woman started the day by freshening up and putting her hair into French braids. She wanted to be cute but not too sexy. She figured that instead of wearing leggings and a crop top to work out like she normally would, she'd switch up.

She had soft biker shorts and a T-strap shirt with a dumbbell on it. She put on her sneakers and grabbed her workout bag, and headed to the gym.

"Nice to meet you, Carly," Ivan said, shaking her hand.

"Nice to meet you too, Ivan," she said, trying not to get lost in his eyes.

He pulled his long hair into a man bun and started with high energy.

"All right! So I read what you want to work on, and there are a few machines and techniques we'll use today. Our workout is 30 minutes long with 15 minutes of stretching after."

During the workout, they got to know each other. She mentioned that her kids were at camp, and she had the house all to herself this summer.

"I know that feels nice to have a house to yourself,"

he said. "My lease with my roommate ends in 30 days, and I look forward to having my own place."

For the next thirty minutes, he helped her try different workouts and machines, and she was surprised to find that she had the stamina to keep up with him.

Carly loved how encouraging he was every step of the way. The man was attentive, never looking at his phone. Many women looked at him, but he focused on Carly and answered every question she had.

Ivan didn't show it, but he was checking her out the whole time. He thought she was beautiful.

She resembled Constance Wu and probably didn't need his services, but he was glad she was there. She controlled her breathing very well while exercising, and he wanted to hear that same breathing if his dick was in her mouth.

At the end of the workout, Ivan put his hands on her to help her stretch out.

She didn't think she would make it through the stretches because she was so horny. He was respectful and kept his hands where they needed to be, but he kept eye contact with her during each stretch.

His body weight was on her when he stretched her leg and ass muscles.

He would occasionally ask, "Is this okay? Is this too much for you?"

His tone was professional, but her mind was definitely in the gutter. She even felt her nipples get hard, and she thought she squirted during two of the stretches.

Ivan told her the stretches were hamstring and calf stretch, hip opener, and finally, the adductor/inner thigh stretch.

After the workout, he helped her up and told her it was refreshing working with her.

"I look forward to going a little harder at the next session," he said.

Carly damn near drooled when she heard him say that.

She thanked him for the session, and when she got home, she ran to her room to masturbate. She was thankful her kids weren't home.

She didn't even need lubricant; she was wetter than the gym's pool. She knew she came faster when she was reclined, so she threw a large towel on the floor and lay on her back before stretching her pussy lips apart with two fingers.

She did that a few times before inserting her fingers in herself. She pulled her fingers out, and she definitely had her juices coating them.

She plunged them back in as she thought about Ivan hovering over her during one of the stretches and heard him in her head encouraging her to push through it. Her mind was racing, and she knew she was close.

She used her fingers to gently rub on her clit. She was starting to breathe faster.

She worked on switching between the two places and even fondled her own breasts before she lost touch with reality for a bit before she settled into a moment of intense pleasure.

She felt herself come back to reality about thirty seconds later.

She grabbed her messy towel to clean her fingers and headed for the shower.

* * *

Today was Wednesday and Carly's second workout with Ivan. She was stoked and looking forward to working out with him. Her outfit today was an athletic jumpsuit.

Carly couldn't tell, but Ivan wanted to smack her ass. It looked perfectly shaped in the outfit. She sweated a little more during today's workout, and he could only imagine what it would be like to see her sweating after a sex session.

He cleared his thoughts when he heard her say, "There go, my friends."

She waved to the women.

He could see them across the gym giggling but focused on Carly.

"Your friends seem nice," he said as they walked to their next machine.

"They're all right. We're all moms, so it feels good being around other women every once in a while."

Then she admitted that there was a bet between them about which one could bed him first.

"Are you serious?" he said. "I feel like a piece of meat."

The two laughed before starting the machine.

As usual, he motivated her while she worked out.

"I'll pay you $100 to make it look like you're flirting with me," she offered.

"Carly. Your friends will get a kick out of that," he said.

"Did you drive here?" she asked.

He was confused. "Yes."

"I want you to drive me off in your car," she said.

"You're wicked," he said as he continued to assist her.

It wasn't long before the two finished their workout and set up for the stretching session.

The women watched in awe as he did the same stretches as last time.

Carly liked that Ivan flirted with her a bit during the stretch. She was just as horny as last time, and she still squirted during the stretches.

But when they finished stretching, he helped her up. She loved seeing the women's jealous faces.

"I'm not a slut or anything," she told him as they walked out the doors of the gym.

Jackie and Tanya ran to the door to watch them leave together.

"I never thought you were," Ivan said.

"I just want to win the bet," she said once they reached her car.

Her phone was receiving all kinds of messages, and she assumed it was Jackie and Tanya. She wanted to gloat, but she was conversing with Ivan.

"This is so unprofessional, but I would love to help you," he said. "I'd be lying if I said I didn't want to go to bed with you."

She couldn't believe he'd said that. She looked him in his eyes and stated, "Are you serious?"

He told her he was. He admitted he'd had a sexual relationship with a client a few months ago. It had gone south, but he felt like being with Carly would be different.

"You're the ideal MILF," he told her.

"Ivan!" she exclaimed.

She didn't like being called that. This wasn't a porno.

He apologized and said he would still actually love to fuck her.

"We have the chemistry," he said, kissing her before driving his car to the side of the parking lot where she was parked. "Keep the $100!" he told her. "Treat me like a slut."

They arrived at her car, and she thanked him.

When he pulled off, and she got into her vehicle, all she could think was, *What did I get myself into?*

* * *

That night, Carly did video calls with her kids. Afterward, she was preparing for bed when she received a message from Ivan.

> Since you want to win the bet, my last workout tomorrow is at 6 p.m. I dare you to meet me at my place at 7. I know you have the stamina for me to work you out in bed.

543 Camelot Dr

Apt 12

She couldn't stop smiling at the message. It made her warm all over, but all she responded with was, I'll think about it.

* * *

The next morning, she was still mulling over the idea. She ran her errands and didn't hear from the gossiping two.

She told them she had been sexting with Ivan. They didn't believe her.

While she texted them, she received a text message from Ivan.

It was an image of his dick print in his workout clothes.

The message said, *Thinking about you.*

Her eyes looked at how thick the print was, and her heart started beating faster.

It was 6:30 p.m. when she got out of the shower. Her put on light makeup and dressed in workout clothes, but underneath she had lace lingerie that fit her body well.

Carly decided to accept the dare because she

wanted to win the bet. And it had been years since a man had explored her depths. She needed her cobwebs knocked out.

She reached the bachelor pad he shared with a roommate. Nervously, she knocked on the door. She heard footsteps approaching and couldn't stop smiling when she saw Ivan at the door. He was shirtless, his hair framed his face, and he had a towel wrapped around his hips.

She didn't know he had tattoos on his torso.

Ivan gently grabbed her hand and invited her in.

The apartment was small and reminded her of one she'd had when she first started adulthood about 20 years ago.

"I didn't think you would come," he said. "But my roommate straightened up the living room before he left tonight."

He led her to his room, which was dimly lit. She could still tell it was clean. She was shocked.

Ivan had lit a few candles, and the sweet aroma relaxed her a bit. There was a wine bottle in the room with plastic wine glasses.

Carly didn't know why, but she liked that he'd put in the effort.

She cleared her throat when he sat on the edge of the bed and asked her to sit next to him. Her heart was racing like a Nascar vehicle. She sat next to him, and he noticed she didn't seem like herself.

"Are you okay?" he said, holding her hand and looking into her eyes.

"I've only been with two men in my life," she said. "My kids' fathers. I haven't had sex in about two years. And now seeing you in the towel makes me realize this is real."

"You bit off more than you could chew?"

His choice of words put a smile on her face, and she said, "Exactly."

"I mean, I was going to get dressed, but you knocked on the door before I could," he said.

"No need to make you get dressed for what we're doing tonight," she said, leaning in for a kiss.

Ivan leaned in and completed it. He expected the kiss to be chaste, and it was just that.

"We can stop right here," he said, pulling away.

"Hell no," she said thinking about his picture from earlier. "I need to know what that dick feels like."

"Come find out then," he said, lying on his back.

She climbed on top of him and could still feel him through the towel. She kissed him a bit more passionately, and he instantly placed his hands on her ass.

The two kissed like it was their last time together. She kissed each of his tattoos. While she was on top of him, he kissed her lips harder and started fingering her from behind.

She gasped in between kisses.

He was so glad he was getting this opportunity. He'd always wanted to fuck a mother.

Ivan used his fingers deftly, and she rocked herself on them. He was about to add a third when he felt her pussy muscles contract around them.

She came and crashed her lips against his. She still bounced on his fingers until he slowly pulled them out.

Ivan was rock hard now. She climbed down his body and undid the towel. His dick sprang up, and she knew that thing could do damage.

It was the length of her arm.

He watched her confidently grasp it and put it in her mouth. She heard him protest that he didn't need head, but she did it anyway.

"Pretty lady," he said while watching her mouth move on him, "I have to get a condom."

That brought Carly to reality.

How could she forget condoms? She had packed an overnight bag with a vibrator. She had been so worried about looking cute and whether she should actually do this, but she hadn't even thought of condoms.

Ivan reached over to his bedside table and grabbed one. She was thankful he had some.

"I usually come fast," he said, securing it on. "But condoms help me last longer."

"I come fast, too," she said. "Especially if I'm on my back."

This was information Ivan was glad to have.

He watched as she climbed on top of him. She looked sexy as hell on top of him, and he kissed her softly. Their kiss intensified as she gripped his dick and put the tip in.

Ivan closed his eyes in bliss at how well they united.

She bounced on the tip until she felt comfortable giving herself the rest. Even though she was wet, Ivan felt like she was still tight.

He was going to ask if she was okay, but she spoke up first.

"Stretch me just like that," she said.

She was pleased with him for letting her control her movements because she knew she would come faster on her own.

"Use me however you want," he said.

Ivan knew it wasn't his imagination how good it felt to be inside of her. He felt like he was slipping inside a wet, soft, hot nest meant just for him. He felt like he belonged inside of her.

He loved hearing her moan as she worked herself to her peak. She looked so damn sexy as she told him she was about to come.

Carly felt an electric energy running through her body. She could feel her heartbeat in her pussy, and finally, she felt a thunderous feeling over her body. She felt goosebumps and tingles down her spine.

Ivan continued stroking her pussy with his dick and felt her body tremble from it.

He flipped them over because he wanted to see her come fast on her back.

He treated the moment like a stretching session at the gym, wrapping one of her legs around his waist and pushing the other into her chest as he gave her medium strokes with only half of his length.

He never lost eye contact with her, and it made the experience even more erotic.

He could hear her pacing her breathing as he stroked her. She met his strokes with her own before rubbing her clit.

The room was full of their natural sounds, and she loved it.

Ivan eventually lifted them off the bed and fucked her standing up. He kissed her in this position, and she squirted on his dick.

Her walls contracting against him, he put her back

on the bed and gave long strokes so she could feel all of his length.

She went crazy at this and said, "Just like that!" She looked like she was going to cry from the sensation, and that's when he nutted.

In the same way he motivated her in the gym, she motivated him by saying, "Keep that nut flowing. Don't let it stop."

For the rest of the night, they had an amazing sexual experience. She couldn't believe it was with someone 20 years younger than her!

He even liked her using the vibrator when he was inside of her.

It was midnight when she left.

"You packed an overnight bag. Please just stay," he said.

"You act like you're not going to see me tomorrow for workout number three."

"Shit," he mumbled. "We just had workout number three."

She protested that she needed to go home because she had plans before the workout.

To his dismay, they parted ways.

As soon as she got in the car, she did her "Happy Girl" and her "Bitch! You-Just-Got-You-Some" dances. She didn't want to embarrass herself doing that at his place.

* * *

The next day while at the gym preparing for her workout with Ivan, she saw Jackie and Tanya.

"You ladies owe me a day of relaxation," she told them.

"You boned him?" Jackie asked.

"Girl! He had me coming all night."

"I don't believe you," Tanya said.

All three women went to the bathroom in the biggest stall, and she showed them the hickeys on her neck and on her breasts.

Ivan approached the women who didn't seem to believe Carly. He hugged her, something they never saw him do with clients.

He grabbed her ass and said, "You're one hot MILF."

This time hearing it, she loved it.

The two women couldn't believe it.

Ivan kissed Carly on the cheek, and Carly stuck her tongue out at her friends.

She liked being his MILF.

Be Kind, Rewind
By Jade St. James

"BABY. THIS STORE IS OUTDATED," CHRISTINE said to her husband Bixby.

The man agreed with her and said, "This is definitely retro."

"But it's still cute though."

The married couple had just enjoyed a great dinner and several drinks. They weren't ready to go home yet and found themselves in an old-fashioned porn store, wandering through the aisles, laughing and having a good time while they waited for their Uber.

The establishment had posters of porn stars from the early 2000s, the dildos looked average, the selection of vibrators was more battery-operated than electric, the lingerie was basic, and then there were DVDs.

"What'd you know," he said, looking at the long

aisle of DVDs. "Who even knew you could still get porn on DVD?"

Christine started laughing. Bixby figured she was laughing at how retro the store was and not because she had liquor in her system.

The two laughed at the names of the DVDs, "Kelly the Coed," "Island Fever," "Big, Black, and Beautiful," and "Black College Coed."

"Our DVD player still work?" Bixby asked.

Christine looked at her husband with the what-are-you-thinking look.

"Yes," she replied.

"Why don't we buy one of these and role-play the first scene?"

"Look at you being adventurous," she said. "Plus, I want to fuck you tonight. It's been a few days."

His eyes twinkled at her response. Her eyes gleamed when her eyes met his.

"Christine," he said. "You pick the movie and whatever the couple does in the first scene... we have to do. No chickening out."

She laughed, "Make sure you don't chicken out!"

"Our Uber will be here in seven minutes," he told her as she roamed the DVDs.

Her goal was to choose a video where not only he found the leads attractive, but she did too.

Five minutes passed by before her husband said their ride was two minutes away.

"Perfect!" She said. "Because I found the right one for us."

Christine picked a DVD called "Ladies First."

Bixby couldn't lie. The woman on the cover looked like she demanded attention, and he hoped tonight Christine would do the same.

The two checked out and stood outside for their Uber.

In the Uber home, they giggled and groped each other. The driver could hear their smooching sounds, and he chuckled under his breath. The two would occasionally read the back of the case. Christine's hands rubbed over Bixby's crotch to feel his hard dick. He was leaving hickeys on her neck. They were trying not to let their driver know how horny they were, but they didn't do a very convincing job.

He knew the couple was having fun, and he wasn't going to judge them.

When they arrived home, they ran to the den. It contained the only DVD player in the house.

They were already naked by the time Bixby pressed play.

Without any story, the scene begins with a woman on all fours, and a man behind her eating her out.

"Foreplay already? Now that's what I'm talking about." Christine said, seeing the couple in action on television.

Bixby gripped his dick and started stroking himself.

The couple looked at the screen again and then looked at each other.

"Assume the position!" Christine exclaimed.

The den sofa had a blanket, and she threw it on the floor with pillows. She placed her knees on one of the pillows and got on all fours.

This position made her ass look fuller, and Bixby couldn't help but smack it. Her arch was perfect. He placed the other pillow under his knees and started working.

His large hands gripped her ass cheeks and spread them apart as his lips started to kiss her sensitive pussy lips.

She gasped softly as his warm mouth kissed her bottom set of lips. Her eyes closed in ecstasy as one of his favorite muscles entered her folds – that muscle was his tongue.

He was meticulous as his tongue and lips worked interchangeably to pleasure her.

"Fuck," she mumbled in between her moans.

This experience felt like he was massaging her

pussy with his mouth. It felt luscious, delicious, and luxurious as he did so. Periodically, he rubbed circular motions on her ass cheeks.

"I'm about to cum," she said.

She needed access to her clit, so she lay on her back as she felt him continue to pleasure her. This new position allowed her to gently rub her clit.

Bixby didn't change his motions. He was shocked she was about to cum. She hasn't cummed from foreplay in months.

Christine had to admit. This was the definition of sit back, relax, and enjoy. He moved her fingers out of the way and started focusing on her clit as he fingered her.

"Oh my God!" She exclaimed repetitively.

She couldn't put her finger on the right words. Still, this irresistible, pleasant pressure rose up into her belly until she clenched the blanket into her hands and let out a massive groan.

Her orgasm felt so good she told him, "Don't stop."

He obliged and let her fuck his tongue until she stopped herself. He pulled away from her and paid attention to his dick.

He glanced at the television screen; the couple on the screen were in a different position.

Bixby used the video as inspiration to get harder. He and Christine watched as the woman in the flick was now riding the man.

Christine grinned big and wasted no time.

"Giddy up," she said as she hovered her pussy over his dick.

She lined up his dick with her pussy. She rubbed his tip between her folds to get him slick and slowly slid down him.

"Fuck!" She hissed as she felt her pussy adjust to his dick. Bixby cursed at the feeling of entering her.

Christine used the next five minutes to rock herself on his stiffness. She could not believe how in sync they were and didn't want to let the feeling go. She rode him like a horse, and he didn't complain.

The cacophony of their moans and groans bounced off the den walls. Then, finally, Bixby came in her.

She wasn't upset. She knew he came fast, and she was okay with it. But she knew her orgasm was soon to come.

While he came off his high, she did Kegels on him.

The couple were so wrapped up into each other they didn't realize the couple on the DVD had changed positions.

In the next 20 minutes, they match the porn stars as they change positions.

Christine could not believe how cohesive she and Bixby were tonight because of the video. She thought to herself that they needed to do this more often.

"Wait!" Bixby exclaimed. "Is his tongue in her butt?"

"Yep. Get in there, hon!"

"Yes, ma'am," he said. "I have to make a pit stop first."

She was confused as her husband left the den and headed somewhere else in the house. She stimulated her pussy while waiting; she didn't want her pussy to get dry. A few moments later, she saw him arrive with a butt plug they hadn't used in months.

"Oh hell yeah," she said as he joined her on the floor.

Once again, the woman got on all fours, and Bixby wasted no time eating her ass. She actually enjoyed it. She didn't think she would.

She called out his name as he worked on her. They worked together as he inserted the plug in her. He eased it in there based on her comfort levels.

"Fuck me, missionary, please," she said as she rubbed her clit and felt the plug work magic. "I'll be coming soon."

Bixby didn't waste any time.

He placed his hands on her breasts as leverage as he slid his dick into her warm pussy.

"Damn. You warmer than a fresh apple pie."

Christine couldn't lie; she enjoyed that compliment, but having him inside of her was even more ravishing.

His sex strokes were soft, gentle, and sweet.

"Don't make love to me," she told him. "Fuck me."

Bixby didn't even need inspiration from the DVD to fuck Christine. He didn't have to match the man in the video. He knew Christine liked to be choked while he did fast, hard strokes.

He watched as she matched his movements. She talked him into choking her lightly, and she looked to be in pure bliss as he did this.

He wrapped her legs around his waist and went to town on her. His dick was hard as hell, and he fit into her like a puzzle piece.

Her mouth made the perfect o-shape. She knew he loved when she made that love face.

His strokes were making her dizzy – in a good way. It felt good having him inside of her. She wanted him in her all night.

His hands gripped her hips as he thrust into her more. It was tantalizing being touched by him.

She knew they were going to fuck hard until she came. She was all for that orgasmic feeling.

He felt like a surfer riding the waves in her pussy, and he was going to release soon, but he needed her to climax first.

"I'm almost there," she managed to screech out, and he loved knowing she was near.

He released his grip from around her neck. She wrapped her legs around him more. It wasn't by her doing, but Christine found herself climaxing at exactly the same moment as the woman on the DVD.

Bixby watched as her face changed into a smile, and she was trying to catch her breath. He lived to see her in pure bliss like that.

Bixby slowly pulled out of her and started stroking her clitoris.

She started squirming and quivering. Her pussy was so sensitive after her climax.

He did a soft chuckle at her actions. He started stroking his dick and said, "I'm going to nut."

"Please, baby on my stomach," she said.

The couple instantly got distracted by the couple on the screen. The female lead sounded so alluring as she and the male lead worked together to get him to his climax.

The two watched as the man in the scene straddled the woman on the ground. It was obvious he was going to jerk his load on the beautiful woman's face.

"I know you don't like that," Bixby said to Christine. "I'll listen to your request and do this on your stomach."

"The rules of the game are clear, babe. Cum on my face."

Bixby was ready to do it. But he couldn't believe how open she was being tonight. He was, too, but this was nice to see her do this tonight.

Bixby placed himself back in Christine to get more strokes. Instead of making love to her, he fucked her to get himself to the climax faster.

While he used quicker movements, she used kegels on him again.

"I love watching you fuck me," she said, looking down at his dick working inside of her. "I can't wait for you to cum on my face."

Bixby usually didn't need motivation, but it was inspiration he didn't know felt so damn good. It was an ego boost that made this moment better.

Christine felt like she was going to cum again, but she remained focused on Bixby.

She knew he was close because his strokes were getting harder. She thought she could feel him at the bottom of her pussy.

"I'm about to cum," he said through clenched teeth as he pulled himself out of her.

He straddled his wife and stroked his dick to land his load on her face.

"Fuck! Fuck! Fuck!" He exclaimed as his white substance covered her face.

"Yes, baby!" She exclaimed as the hot, sticky load covered her face. A few drops hit her lips, and she used her tongue to grab them so she could indulge in the taste of her husband.

"Shit!" He said as he pushed his tip in her mouth, and she sucked it hard.

His body shook for a few seconds before he removed himself from his beautiful wife's mouth.

As the couple collected themselves, they looked to the screen and saw the woman lick her finger and shove it in the man's ass.

Christine said, "I know you don't like that."

"The rules of the game are clear, babe. Put a finger in me."

The couple rewound the DVD and watched how they reached that point. The woman gave the man head before finger-fucking the man.

"Get on your back, Bixby," she told him.

Bixby got on his back, and Christine gave him head. Her lips were the side character as they worked on the main character: his dick and balls. Her hands made a cameo appearance to aid in getting Bixby comfortable.

Explicit words and moans escaped his mouth as his wife worked on him.

She pushed his knees into his chest to get access to his asshole. She watched him stroke his own dick in this position. Then she licked her index finger before sliding it into his ass. She did so while massaging his bones.

His dick was so slippery from her mouth.

"Not bad," he said as she worked her hand on his balls and finger in his ass. "I don't mind this baby," he said.

Christine couldn't believe he was moaning at this.

"Should I add a finger?" She asked.

"No," he told her. "But keep this up. I'm about to cum," he said.

She continued to work the one finger and her hand, but he told her to move her hands.

She did as she was told. Bixby sat up, stroked his dick, and told her, "Put it in your mouth."

The woman engulfed his dick in her mouth.

Without warning, she felt the cum enter her mouth, and she swallowed every last drop as he came.

"Fuck Christine," he said through gritted teeth as he removed himself from her mouth.

The woman was pleased with herself. They hit new sexual limits tonight, and it was invigorating.

He pulled her on top of his body, and the couple cuddled with her through the night.

* * *

Two weeks later, the couple has a Saturday of nothing to do.

"We need to go to the adult store," Christine said.

"Another night of role play?"

"Oh yes," she said. "This time, you pick the DVD and costume for me to wear."

Bixby was so interested.

The two drove to the store and headed right towards the DVD section for their Saturday role-play.

Afterword

Well, what did you think of this new collection?

I'd be thrilled if you could take one minute to leave a review. And leave any feedback you have! I read every review.

Thanks so much for going on this "hardcore" ride with me. I hope you enjoyed it as much as I did.

All my love and respect,
Jade